THE LONGEST MEMORY

By the same author

Poetry
MAMA DOT
AIRY HALL
BRITISH SUBJECTS

Plays
A JAMAICAN AIRMAN FORESEES HIS DEATH

THE LONGEST MEMORY

A NOVEL

Fred D'Aguiar

PANTHEON BOOKS, NEW YORK

Library of Congress Cataloging-in-Publication Data
D'Aguiar, Fred, 1960–
The longest memory/Fred D'Aguiar.
p.   cm.
ISBN 0-679-43962-5
1. Virginia—History—1775–1865—Fiction. 2. Afro-American men—
Virginia—Fiction. 3. Fathers and sons—Virginia—Fiction.
4. Slaves—Virginia—Fiction. I. Title.
PR 9320.9.D 34 L66 1995
813—dc20   94-28276
CIP

Manufactured in the United States of America

First American Edition
2 4 6 8 9 7 5 3 1

For Debbie

I have been in Sorrow's kitchen and licked out all the pots.

Zora Neale Hurston

unless
You become acquainted now
With each refuge that tries to
Counterfeit Atlantis, how
Will you recognize the true?
W. H. Auden

CONTENTS

REMEMBERING

The future is just more of the past waiting to happen. You do not want to know my past nor do you want to know my name for the simple reason that I have none and would have to make it up to please you. What my eyes say has never been true. All these years of my life are in my hands, not in these eyes or even in this head. I woke up one day before the estate stirred, tiptoed over my workmates, former playmates and bedfellows and everything else to do with robbed intimacy, unlatched the door, confronted a damp, starlit morning and decided that from this day I had no name. I was just boy, mule, nigger, slave or whatever else anyone chose to call me. I have been called many other things besides. My eyes are bloodshot and rheumy. I have not been crying: I don't do that anymore. The last time I cried was over the pointless death of a boy I loved as my own. I swore it would be the last time because it hurt more than any pain I'd felt before or since. I never knew crying could take over a body so, rock it, shake it, rattle it, thump it so that the body feels wrecked and cries without tears or movement of any kind, out of sheer exhaustion, except for that moan, groan, hoarse, bass wail. That was me over the whipping of a boy who had to know better somehow and would have learned with a good talking to, or even a beating in these circumstances but not this, not this. I don't want to remember. Memory hurts. Like crying. But still and deep. Memory rises to the skin then I can't be touched. I hurt all over, my bones ache, my teeth loosen in their gums, my nose bleeds. Don't make me remember. I forget as hard as I can.

1

WHITECHAPEL

That morning I faced the world for the first time as a nobody, nameless. Because I had no name I was able to return to my body-shaped space on the straw mat on the floor, clear a few limbs out of the way and sleep so deep I was the last to rise, when before I'd lie there and listen to the others breathe, snore, talk in their sleep, cry out, whimper, shield their heads from a blow, contract their bodies to receive a lash, kick and punch as if bloodhounds were upon them, grind their teeth so loud it sounded like two huge stones rubbed together, whinny like horses and bray like mules, grunt like hogs, howl like wolves, or just plain die with a gasp.

I did this going to sleep last and waking first routine for too long. The bags under my eyes are sacks of worries, witnesses of dreams, nightmares and sleep from which a man should not be allowed to wake. The last breath is not exhaled as the body releases its hold on life and the bones relax into the shape of sleep. That's wrong. The last breath is fought for. Air is sucked in. The chest heaves and swells with the effort. The eyes are flung open as the dreamer realizes this dream of death is real and his last. He literally wakes from sleep startled that this breath is final and instead of relief he registers fear more akin to surprise. Had he been prepared by some marvelous counsel, then he would have welcomed this last breath as if he were being fed honey and died with his eyes closed and a smile on his lips. But the fight for air instills panic. The thing we have talked over countless times as our only salvation creeps up on us and catches us by surprise. All the laughing we did over it becomes the last laugh. Death's last laugh. My feeling is mixed. The breath should have been mine. Why must I be the witness to something I deserve more than anyone on this plantation? I've seen enough for one life, several lives. I forget if I've dreamed an experience or really remember it. I put most recollection down to fantasy. That boy of mine was not whipped to death for running away, for getting nowhere, not even to the next town. He jumped into my head in a whipping scene because I'd sat through too many to recall with exact order and sat because each stroke of the whip buckled my legs from under me and drained me of every ounce of my energy just to watch without sound with my hand over my eyes. If I look away I risk inviting a beating. So I look with these blood-shot eyes that see without seeing, witness without registering a memory or sensation. The boy's two hundred lashes lasted no more than twenty minutes but he was gone half-way into it all. I saw when he switched from screaming at each blow, tensing his body for the next, screaming on impact again, relaxing his body for a moment to catch his breath and groan and then tensing again. Sometimes he would tense too late. The whip seemed to cause the nerves to tighten as if it imbued the body with life rather than draining that life away. His screams were louder then and simultaneously a little weaker than before. That's when I learned how to live without being hurt by life, sensation, this witnessing of things taxing. I literally saw the boy surrender to that whip, those blows, the whole rhythm of lash, pause, lash and tense, breathe, tense. I saw it in his eyes. They looked at me, at us all, for one last time, and clouded, misted, glazed themselves. For the rest of the beating we begged with greater intensity and risk to ourselves for him to be spared because we had all seen him cross from our world to the next, but when his name was called he always answered clearly and nodded, which was taken as good grounds to resume the punishment. The whip ate into him, but like all gluttons who have gorged themselves to their fill, it bit and chewed without swallowing and simply bit and chewed some more, until its mouth was so full that food seeped out its corners to make room for more. The whip fed on him until the count reached two hundred. We cut him down and called his name throughout and he found something somewhere to nod and answer just as before but his look was distant, removed from the events perpetrated on his body, not in the least bit interested in our fuss and worry and open grief for him. I took on his look from that moment. We dressed his back with balm that took away feeling and stopped blood in its tracks. We talked to him and he nodded, but he stopped answering to his name. Then his head hardly moved, then not at all, and his eyes which remained the same told us nothing. That's how I know he was gone half-way into that beating when he stopped screaming 'father' because he could see I was being held down and was no good to him. The eyes became less wide and still and the tears that continued to stream from them did so in a steady flow, whereas before they seemed to appear in floods as the whip tore into him. I closed those eyes after one last look at them. I said sorry and closed them and turned away from them into their exact look in my own eyes. I was crying up till then, uncontrollably during the whipping, then as I tended his back, almost noiselessly, in order to steady my hand whose touch made his flesh recoil. 'My hand is not the whip son,' I said or imagined saying to him. He nodded to everything, then nothing. I had to have no name to match this look and the remainder of this life.

Sour-face, they call me. There are lines, two of

them, on each side of my mouth, turned-down lines, two short strokes that run from the corner of my lips down my chin, as deep as any scar but earned over nights of lying awake staring at the dark and the dark staring back, unblinkingly, and listening to the hut turning in its sleep, and then hearing the turns without thinking, 'turn', because the looking and listening had become numb and the brain had emptied itself, gone numb too as a result of so much hard attention to nothing and everything. I feel a trickle of saliva unburdening along the left sour line at the side of my mouth. A little trickle on wheels relocating to a more joyful place. My hand should come up to my face, and swipe it out of existence. But I think of the action, see it even, and nothing happens. So the trickle continues over my chin and along the stubble of my neck, slowing down and reducing in size as each inch of the trail it leaves behind subtracts from its mass. Worry cut those paths in my face. I let it happen because I didn't feel it happening and only knew it was there when someone called me Sourface one day and I looked in the mirror for evidence and found plenty staring back at me.

What was I before this? I forget. Did I smile? Laugh out loud? Don't recall. To laugh. What is that? I think of a donkey braying. That is like a big laugh, involuntary, involving the whole body, noisy and long and toothy. What could lead to such behavior? There is nothing in my past to make me bray. Knowing this, I can say I will never laugh again, if I ever did. Sour-face, that's me. Not Dead-eyes. Not Black-head. Not Ancient, though I've earned ancient. But Sour-face. The lines were chis-elled there without my permission. I must have worried and called it by another name. Like think-ing. How else could I have done it for so long with-out worrying that I was doing something that would exact a toll on me? Thinking things over I see now how I made my life harder than it needed to be and longer than necessary.

My face says life is sour. A life that was fresh to begin with but one left out too long turned to this: counting the hours that drag through the dark, bid-ing the minutes that hop and shift and hobble along the days. When I lie still at night I am those hours re-fusing to pass. Getting around the plantation one of those minutes has a sour face and returns my sour mouth inside the rim of a cup of water.

I have buried two wives and most of my children. I am surrounded by grandchildren and great grand-children. They think I am a Judas and an old man who can make a great pepper stew when goaded to do so. They leave me alone most of the time, fuss over me from a suitable distance at meal times, check to see if I am still alive first thing in the morning with a tug or a prod, then disappear for the day into the fields.

One of them ran into me once. We both rounded

the same corner of the house thinking it was a river flowing one way. I was going at my minute pace, he was running full pelt from a stick wielded by someone with authority over him. He knocked me off my feet and I rolled for several yards before stopping face up in the stars. He carried on running and the stick bearer came over to me and helped me to my feet then whacked me on the legs for delaying him, before resuming the chase. That knock that brought out stars in broad daylight recurs. I walk far from corners I can't see around, though I've never met anyone in that way since. Suddenly I'll be stopped in my tracks by a knock in my head and the stars will come out and if I can't reach out and hold something to steady me I'll slump down on the ground for my own good or keel over. At first they, the great grandchildren, fussed over me and argued I was done for, but I always recovered so fast they left me alone. My great grandchildren started calling me Sit-down Grandfather. I liked that more than Sour-face. Sometimes when I saw one coming, I'd wait until I was sure they saw me, and then I'd sit down deliberately, as if the stars had forced me off my feet, and when the look of worry and alarm made them dart to me, I'd wave them away impatiently. They would laugh. I mean like a donkey. I can't laugh, so I'd shake my head at their pleasure and at how easy a-laugh came to them.

Perhaps I laughed with my first wife and

daughters, and my second wife and our son, if not with their children and children's children. They laugh at me. There is no evidence in my eyes to show me that I laughed at any point in my past and certainly nothing in my twisted mouth. A nose is neutral. A nose gives little away, betrays nothing. The temper in a flared nostril might be a warning never to tease that person but it does not say that the bearer of flared nostrils once did something cruel or murderous. Not so with my eyes and mouth. They telegraph my past, my present and my future. Sour-face; dead eyes. Do not meet him at a blind corner. If you do, carry on running, do not hesitate or look back at those eyes, that mouth. Run as if from a big stick. Sour mouth is contagious. Dead eyes turn to stone. Run, even if you share the blood of those eyes, words of that mouth. Eyes that have seen all, mouth that has said nothing but kept silence. Sit-down Grandfather. Laughing stock. Obstacle. Burden, soon. When the red eyes blacken. When the stars I see are from a knock that recurs and the sky is close and black, always black. When I sit it will be for no one but myself. I will not rise and dust my pants off and shake my head at the pleasure given to someone else at my expense. My wife will call and I will answer her the one way I know how, in silence and with a gesture. Now that we speak across the years, without words, across the darkness of this life and her death. She asks me to hold her. But she was already too heavy with death for my arms. The pillows behind her head and back were compressed by her dying over weeks. A slow death that took so long I willed it to come, get its work done and get out of my life. My son held her for me. He looked away to hide his wet eyes. I leaned to her with my ears brushing her nose and mouth to hear her last wish. She said, 'Don't keep me waiting too long.' I finished her sentence for her. She got as far as 'too' in her breathy sentence and I said, 'long', but she said nothing in reply and my son looked at us with a jerk of his head and I knew she was dead.

The next dawn he was gone and by dusk that same day, caught, and before night set in, he'd joined his mother with me leaning over him because he was too heavy to hold or cradle as I imagined I must have cradled him when he was young. I promised her I wouldn't be long but I sent my son in my place less than a full day later. Now I can't die because I can't face her blaming me for sending him ahead of me, or in my place, or at all. My years since her death and his are stolen, cowardly, seen through bloody eyes, felt with numbed skin and aching bones, stale aired, black in the sky and hard in the heart and sour in the mouth. When my great grandchild came round that bend at the back of the house and knocked me off my feet and carried on running, it was from the stick as much as to avenge my son on me. That's why I said nothing to him and he nothing to me. I see the stars of that day each time a little longer than before. One day I know I'll see them and they will be the last thing I see and Sit-down Grandfather will be no more and glad because of it, and a smile might turn up my turned-down mouth: something approximating the beginning of a donkey's bray might escape my lips, if anything.

To my mind a simple lesson in obedience was all that my boy required. He needed to know his station sooner rather than too late. I believed some punishment would do him good because it would keep him alive by driving from his wild head, once and for all, any notion of freedom from responsibility. He was born owned by another man, like his father before him, and like his son would be born. This sounds straightforward enough, but from the increasing number of runaways you wouldn't think so. Where do runaways go when they don't get caught? I always pose this question to the young because I can see their dreams as plain as their color and youth on their faces. Paradise is the answer I get from them. Paradise. Damn right, I shout. When they are captured by the trackers they are consigned to paradise, sent there forthwith. Free at last but not free to tell us anything about it. Run from here and you die. My boy listened to my careful reasoning, shook his head negatively but had the grace to keep quiet and walk away. I knew he put my argument down to old age or cowardice or both.

I must have watched him walk away still shaking his head as if to empty it of my words and decided then that he needed to learn for himself. I knew the cost of such a lesson. The risk was obvious to me and yet the schooling in the idea of subservience, obedience, compliance was different for each of us. It was my view that a slave could live a good, long life if he worked hard, and presented to his master the most dignified aspect of himself, in order to reciprocate the same manner from that master, the same civility, fairness and even kindness once the relationship grew warm and cordial. I saw this with these dead eyes of mine when these eyes were living and wild and thirsty for change, for the right to roam at will. I saw too many healthy, kind, funny young men and women disappear from my life. My son would not be one of them. But I realized that day when he shook off my reasoning and restored his own faulty dreams that I would have to save him from himself with a lesson.

I was distracted by the bedridden demise of his young mother. The fever dried her up till she resembled me in years. She was on the verge of this world and the next. She needed constant attention. I was relieved of most of my duties by the master who informed the overseer to allow me time to attend to her needs. Who could get that degree of consideration shown them but someone who had managed to elicit kindness and fairness from another? The talk with my son and my decision receded from my mind. My wife lost all sense of time and was constant in her distress. Her pain from the lower region of her back was severe. I could not convince the master to pay for a physician to look at her but he did argue and convince me that her time had come and not everyone was able to become an old ox like me. This seemed acceptable, so I set about to make her last days comfortable. The hours took their toll. When she died I was exhausted. My son was gone before I missed him. It was out of my hands or so it seemed until I realized unless I did something he would be in paradise with his mother and his broken body left in a gully somewhere to rot. That would have been his fate if I had washed my hands of my responsibility to him. I could not. The overseer had left with a party of hungry men some hours before in pursuit. He did not even bother to question me. As soon as I heard my son was gone, my only son, the son I'd reasoned with and who had rejected my reasoning, I knew what I had to do.

There are two types of slave: the slave who must experience everything for himself before coming to an understanding of anything and he who learns through observation. The slave in the first category behaves as if he is the only slave in the world and is visited by the worst luck on earth. That type of slave is agitated, brings much trouble on his head and he makes the lot of every slave ten times worse. It is generally accepted that the slave in the second category is brighter, lives longer, causes everyone around him a minimum of worries and earns the small kindness of the overseer and the master. I realized my son was in the first, troublesome category, that day he walked away from my advice. A bolt of lightning shot through my heart. My heartbeat rattled like the start of rain on a roof before steadying again with the rhythm of a downpour.

I resolved to save my son, not to abandon him to the horrible fate he might bring on himself. The news that he had run some hours earlier brought me to the master's front door, the door to his two private rooms upstairs in his house, for the first time in my life. Mr Whitechapel emerged half-dressed, surprised at my boldness and irritated and intrigued by it at the same time. He assumed his customary pose: left hand on his hip, right hand cradling a pipe that jutted from his mouth like an extra organ. I begged his pardon, wished God's blessings on him and his two sons and one daughter and good wife, and proceeded to explain my solution to my son's impulsive idiocy. He cut me short and asked me what I would have him do with a runaway among his good negroes, poisoning their minds on a daily basis. I said that he need not worry about my son because my proposal would ensure a compliant, obedient servant who had made one impulsive indiscretion. He asked again what I would have him do. I looked at him for the first time in our exchange. He was distracted and exasperated. He had never been like this with me before in all the years I had served him. I said I would pray for him and his family as I have always prayed. I begged him to send a man after the search party to ensure my son's safe return and just punishment. He said events were now out of his control and in God's hand. God was just and fair and he and I should accept His judgment on us all. I agreed and took a breath to plead my case but he interceded with the question: Did I seek to contradict his assessment? I said no and again took a breath to reason this dilemma to a fair conclusion. Again he interrupted me by repeating his question, this time with more volume and a degree of anger that was clearly intended to silence me. I bowed. He turned on his heels and I spoke.

'Sir, I know where my son is.'

This stopped him and spun him around to bring him face to face with me as before.

'Where? Where? Where, man? Speak up!'

He was furious and appeared to judge my knowledge of my son's whereabouts as some form of power over him, my master. This was cause enough for me to breathe deeply and cherish the air in his quarters that was perfumed and stale in equal parts. I cast my eyes about the room as if the words I wanted to collect were the various items of clothing I saw strewn about the furniture, which would miraculously leap into my head and off my tongue in recognition.

'Hurry up, man. I haven't all day!'

'Sir, my son believes there is a place called, "paradise," on earth. He has gone to find it. He has done what the young reason to be their prerogative because they are blessed with youth, that is, be impetuous and be damned. He is my only son.'

'Where in hell's name is he, Whitechapel?' My name was bellowed out. Footsteps rushed into his room from all ports of entry: house slaves, his wife and children and two guests of the family who were due to leave when my son's disappearance took precedence. It was the first time he'd called me by name for a long time. To use my name in anger was the severest verbal form of disapproval my master could have shown me. For me, it was the verbal equivalent of a whip lash, what we call a tongue-lashing. I winced and bowed as if a whip had boiled the air around my back.

'He has taken the river path. I beg for leniency. He is grieving for his mother.'

'The river? But the trackers have gone North.'

My master gave orders for a man to catch the trackers and redirect them to the river. Mr White-chapel added that my son was not to be harmed in any way since an example would be made of him for all to see and learn by. He turned on his heels once more and I took that to be my dismissal from his sight. It was the best I could hope for, my son's safe return, but the house slaves cast me such disdainful looks you would believe I'd thrown my son to the lions. They knew and loved him from his early years spent around the master's house when his mother was its cook. They did not understand. They had no one to save. Perhaps the house had become theirs as much as the master's. I cast that look back to as many of them as possible until I opened the door into the yard and found I could breathe again. They were breathing the master's expelled air and perfume and had become so accustomed to it that any source drawing upon the master's disapproval received theirs, too. They seemed as angry at me for annoying him as for the fact that I'd betrayed the whereabouts of my son.

All I could do was wait. My master delayed his departure to the North with his family and guests, until the trackers returned with my son. Mr Whitechapel was to accompany them to the next town then return with his second son, William, leaving his wife and young daughter in the capable hands of his elder son, Thomas. I could do nothing but walk about the plantation sticking close to the main road up to the house, along which the party was sure to come bearing my son. The hours passed like an axle driven through mud. The usual sounds of industry around the plantation quietened as everyone listened for the approach of the overseer. Even the wildlife that sometimes made the place a veritable Eden with their cacophony were today flying about soundlessly and trotting through the woods on tiptoe. So it seemed to me with my ears and eyes peeled for a sign, any sign that my son was back and not consigned to a premature paradise.

The master threw up his arms as he emerged from the house with his family and guests. It was early afternoon. He said he could not delay his departure for Fredericksburg with his guests another minute, otherwise they would be on the road in the dark. He issued orders that my son was to be locked up to await punishment when he returned. Those were his parting words to the deputy. This deputy heard the order in the company of four slaves, myself not included. I was the fifth. Why my heart sank then I know now, but at the time I thought my alarm foolish and misplaced. How many times had the master left the plantation having issued orders that were carried out to the letter? Countless. This allayed my fears a little. I also reasoned that the trackers would pass him on the road on their way back and he would tell them in person. Then I remembered that a message had been sent to them to change the course of their pursuit of my son to the path alongside the river, therefore any such meeting was unlikely. Again my heart rattled and I began to pace the main entrance to the plantation. I sought out the deputy to the overseer and repeated the instructions of the master to him. He said he was not deaf and that I would serve my son best if I remembered my place in the affairs of the estate. I bowed and retreated, having no desire to turn him against me since he would be the one at liberty to ensure that my master's orders were carried out.

Dusk crept up on the plantation and stole into the halls and rooms of the buildings and under the canopy of trees. Before I knew it, I was squinting to see past the main gate that was shrouded in shadow. Night insects broke the conspiracy of silence among the natural life that utilizes daylight. I was thankful. They returned routine to the odd day. Best of all was the sound of dogs barking. Worst, too. I wanted to see my son. I knew they were returning for either of two reasons: they had succeeded in apprehending my son or they were forced to call off the hunt because of failing light. God, let it be the first. The dogs' barks grew loud. They seemed to swoop about my head as they barked, the way bats swerve from an object moments before colliding with it. In the distance I could make out a blot. Several of the slaves ran to meet it adding moving parts to that blot. The blot spread and soon I could see that it was made up of several pieces shifting and growing more distinct. Then I recognized one piece because it moved in a way I'd seen countless times before and had stopped noticing because it was so familiar. There was a moment when the piece sprouted arms, legs, a head, a body and in a flicker, the face of my son: open mouthed, tear stained, bruised, but alive. I rushed to him. He turned his body and face away from me and I knew he must have heard I'd given him up.

I was pushed out of the path and would have stood, still pondering his rejection, had it not been for the task of ensuring that my master's orders were obeyed. For here before me was my son in chains, led and dragged in turn like a wild beast of the forest from which he had been plucked. My son, whose dreams were such that he argued his children would be free. His children! I admit he spoke in this rash manner during our exchange when I said that his place in life was the same place occupied by me and available to his children. I countered then that the evidence of 300 years was against his view and ratified mine. He then walked away and shook off my words much as a drenched dog shakes off water.

Here he was paraded for his wrongheadedness, proving he belonged to the type of people who learned through expensive first-hand mistakes. Only I could save him. In my judgement I did save him when I went to the owner of this plantation that runs as far as the eye can see. The owner of every living soul on it, human, animal, plant and mineral. I went to the one person who had the authority to decide whether the day would bring toil, tears or joy to each of us belonging to him simply by snapping his fingers. I got my master to order that my son be spared from all manner of punishment until his return. I did this. I, nameless, Sour-face, Sit-down Grandfather. Yet he turned his back on me. My son.

The overseer fired orders at everyone. I looked for his deputy. He was nowhere in sight. I called on all my relations to find him so that he could confirm the master's orders concerning the well-being of my son. They ran off calling. The overseer, Mr Sanders, asked me what the fuss was about. I said that before he made another move he should hear the master's words from his deputy who was about to be fetched to him. He asked where I thought his deputy would be at this time except where he'd been every night for the last several months. I said nothing but shook my head and searched my brain for a clue to this puzzling question. The slaves came back nearly at once and I could see the answer to the overseer's question on their faces. His deputy had married some months earlier and had taken to disappearing to his wife at their cottage some five miles from the plantation. The master knew nothing of this. As far as he was concerned his overseer's deputy had week-ends to go off the plantation and visit his wife, not every evening. Tonight he'd set off even though the master had issued him specific orders. A slave attached to the house said the deputy had left on the assumption that my son would not be caught, at least not tonight. Mr Sanders muttered something about orders from the master concerning the well-

being of slaves can only come to him second-hand
from his deputy. It would not be in the interest of a
slave to repeat orders detrimental to his comfort. I
said those orders concerning my son were witnessed
by four others besides myself and it was my duty to
inform him of them. He ordered me to shut up or be
lashed. Many other obscenities were uttered by him
into my face. He had cut his foot badly and was in a
degree of pain. Exhaustion from the day's tracking
shadowed his face. But no amount of personal
discomfort merited this kind of exchange with the
most senior slave on the plantation. I carried on talking as if he'd said what a pleasant sunset we have
tonight, for the task at hand was not his politeness to
me, but the fate of my son. He raised his hand and
his knuckles stung my left ear and temple. I stum-
bled, less from the blow than from the fact of it:
some thirty years ago a similar blow was directed at
me and I, a mere slave, got that overseer, Mr Sanders's father in fact, a severe reprimanding from the
previous master, my present master's father. Thirty
years ago. I managed it then, I would do it again. A
silence fell in the yard. My son looked at me and
lunged for Mr Sanders. Three men in the hunting
party restrained him with little effort. They pushed
his head down and forced up both of his bound arms
high behind his back. His exhaustion made him
cooperate. The overseer looked around and a sheet
of shame settled over his head. He lowered his chin

to his chest and muttered a grudging apology and added that I had asked for it since I would not shut up. He asked me what these orders concerning my son might be. I told him. He threw off his shame and donned an armor of rage. He shouted that his entire day had been eaten up with the pursuit of a renegade. He said he'd faithfully returned the criminal to the plantation when others would have disposed of him upon his capture.

'My only reason for bringing back that young nigger is because the boss said he would be made an example of to discourage further runaways. My foot is cut. I am tired and hungry. There is no way this nigger is not going to face the usual punishment for his crime. An example must be set. Not to punish him now in the appropriate way would be an outrage against this entire plantation. I am the overseer. In the absence of the master I do what is best for the plantation. I do not take orders from a nigger. I don't care if you are 100 years old. You are a slave. Now get out of my way, or as God is my witness, I will strap you up next to your son and give you as many lashes for your insolence.'

As many lashes. I had been threatened with the whip. The master would hear of this. Again I stood riveted to the spot as the crowd around my son drifted to the center of the yard where punishments meant to dissuade onlookers from similar activities were staged. My son called his mother. I heard this above the clatter of 250 plantation slaves.

I grabbed the arm of the strongest kin to me, a man close to my son's age, third grandchild of the tenth of my twelve daughters. I told him to run the five miles to the deputy's house since only he could save my son from this public display of savagery. He looked alarmed. I'd forgotten. A slave discovered off the plantation at night was liable to be killed. I told him I would go myself to save my son. He touched my arm, nodded at me and darted into the shadows of the dusk skulking beneath the trees. I watched his back blend with the shadows then melt into them. My son shouted again for his mother. I parted the crowd to get to him.

'She can't come to you my son. I am here for you.'
He saw me and fell silent and dejected. I put myself before Mr Sanders who frowned. 'My son is all I have, sir. Spare him. Let me take his place.'

Mr Sanders laughed aloud, brushed the air in front of his face as if to rid it of a pest and ordered that I be restrained for as long as it took to administer 200 lashes to my son.

When he said the number of lashes an astonished cry rose from the crowd and filled the early evening air. I began to struggle against the grip of two men who simply tightened their hold on me and forced me to my knees. Fires were lit. Each flame conspired with the remaining scraps of light to drive away the ensuing darkness but to no avail. The first lash ripped a hole in my head and I screamed for my son, who fell as silent as the grass and trees. My two remaining daughters cried with their children and grandchildren and begged Mr Sanders for leniency. They begged and cried. The night was torn to ribbons by their grief.

Now when I hear insects at dusk each click, clatter, and croak is the voice of my blood asking for mercy. None was granted. My son, the last fruit of my wife's womb, her joy, was granted none. I who have worked my life for one estate under one family was shown no respect. I was granted none. I killed my son because I wanted him next to me when I died. Just as he had held his heavy mother weighted by death for me to listen to her last breath, he would hold my head to help my last words out.

So it is that my great grandson can knock me down, discard my fallen body, leave me winded and concussed and think nothing of it. Everyone, without exception, blames me for the death of my son. Run into me and kill me. Bludgeon me with a stick, overseer, I am a common slave. There is blood on my conscience. My memory is longer than time. I want to forget. I don't want to see any more. I answer to 'dog'. My great grandchildren run towards me and I sit down to avoid calamity and they laugh. They bray. Sit-down Grandfather or be knocked down. Killer of children. Protector of the worst fate of your people or any people. Is that what I have become? The master of my fate. No longer in need of control or supervision. One so accustomed to his existence that he impinges on his own freedom and can be left to his own devices. A master of his own slavery. Slave and enslaver. Model slave. Self-governing slave. Thinks freedom is death. Thinks paradise is the afterlife. Has practiced death in life for years but death will not come. Sees death in his eyes, in his mouth. Has a body bereft of laughter, sleep, love, purpose. Bestower of death. Outliving all. The eyes seeing them off. The sour mouth fixed in disdain. Eyes and mouth, seeing off a son, ten daughters, several grandchildren, two wives, have nothing left to kill but themselves. The eyes turn on themselves. The mouth sneers at itself. Stare and sneer and (hopefully) die. But no, the mornings repeat after snatched sleep. I scramble over relatives, walk into the quiet light, spreading, without so much as a rustle, over everything and sit facing where the sun starts. The sun begins because it must. When will it die? Will I witness the death? Sun, see me out of this world. I have more family on that other side than on this. Bear me to them. Warm my frozen eyes. Sweeten my mouth. Stir my dead loins. I'll lie down here. Cover me.

2

MR WHITECHAPEL

I leave the plantation for one night and a day, one night and a day, that's all, and I return to virtual chaos. Overseer, you were supposed to supervise. Deputy, you are paid to work for me and do as I say on my plantation. Whitechapel, you may be the most senior man on this plantation but you have overstepped the mark in your recent antics. Your son, God rest his agitated soul, has brought calamity on my head. He is dead through his own design. Thank God my wife and daughter were not present to witness the debacle. His action was rebellion of the most heinous kind. Had he survived, his life on this plantation would have been finished. You yourself have said that a slave who has tasted liberty can never be a proper slave again. You, Whitechapel, agreed with me to contain your son's anarchic spirit. We agreed in this very dining room to protect him from himself by driving from his mind the foolish notions of freedom. Whitechapel, you failed. I trusted you and you disappointed me.

Tell me what I am to do with a plantation of disgruntled slaves. Sell every last man, woman and child if you ask me. That's my inclination. Give you all up to the four corners of these States and see how you fare. My acquaintances tell me I am too lenient. They tell me I fatten up slaves too much with large, regular meals and decent quarters and I work them too little. No, I argue back, on the contrary, a satisfied slave is a happy slave and a more productive worker. Treat them like equals and they respond with nobility. Instead, what do I get, Whitechapel? Reassurances from you and this effrontery from your son. I say his punishment was just, however ramshackle its execution might have been.

Leave us now Whitechapel, we have much to discuss, and let me hear that you have done everything in your power to influence your fellows to comply with the affairs of this plantation. Your son's death is a matter of deepest regret to us all, but in our view he brought it upon himself. He may as well have taken his life with his own hands. You should have saved him from himself, Whitechapel. You were his guardian. Leave us. Remember, were it not for your seniority, there would be charges of insubordination brought against you for your behavior towards Mr Sanders. You owe him an apology. There. Close the door behind you like a good man.

I don't have to watch Whitechapel. It's you two I have to watch. I pay you good money every month but it doesn't seem to be enough to content a deputy. Where were you last night? Your habit of disappearing from the plantation as regularly as was reported to me may have cost you your job. Make the explanation good. Damn good. And my overseer, my right hand man. My eyes and ears and my mouth when I am absent, because I can't be in two places at once, what manner of management do you call the shambles of last night? I am lucky to have returned to a plantation at all. Had I gone North with my wife, my son and my daughter what would I have come back to find? My home burned to the ground and my livelihood ruined, given the level of discontent that you have spread among my slaves. What was going through your head when you heard my orders to hold that rascal until I returned? Did you think you were better schooled in the management of a slaveholding than I? Was it your intention to disobey my orders and come up with a better result? How can I be sure you will ever carry out my careful instructions again without a whim entering your head and causing you to deviate from this or that portion of it because it does not suit you? Or you fail to see the reasoning of it and deem it to be flawed and, therefore, amenable to your reform? Tell me why I should retain you when I can't trust you not to ruin me? Speak man. Where is the tongue that told Whitechapel in no uncertain terms that my orders to hold his son were meaningless in your estimation of the situation? Who gave you the authority? How do you plan to redeem to me the cost of losing a slave in the prime of his working life? I will fine you, Mr Sanders. You will repay to me every last cent of that boy's value. Do you understand? Were it not for the fact that our fathers worked together, you would be relieved of this job, Mr Sanders. I am roundly disappointed in you.

Whitechapel is a good man. He has seen enough death without you taking his only son from him. He deserved better treatment. He knew our fathers for God's sake. He instructed you in the responsibilities of your post. What were you thinking about when you struck him and had his son whipped to death before his eyes? Is that the kind of man you take me for? That I would be pleased with this brutal form of management? Don't you think . . . I cry out of anger and disappointment. My fury will not result in revenge. You must understand. I see from your behavior that the argument of my acquaintances, that slaves should always be shown a stern, distant hand, appears to triumph on my plantation over my own view; a view upheld at considerable expense, and one held, I might add, by my father and your father, that the lot of the slave is miserable enough without being compounded by unnecessary hardships and cruelties. How long do you think that approach would work? These acquaintances – I don't call them friends for this very fact – run estates rife with all forms of rebellious behavior on the part of their pitiable slaves. When is the last time I have had reason to order a public beating of a slave? Only the other week I read in *The Virginian* that a man tried to shoot an apple from the head of his slave at some twenty paces. The terrified slave ran from the man's aim and the man shot him for it. This inhuman display parading as discipline is a regular occurrence on these so-called 'tightly run' operations. I tell you all the evidence supports my belief that as a long-term measure it is a disaster. Contrary to their arguments, such rough handling provides rougher responses. The human spirit is passive in some but nature shows us that it is rebellious in most. Africans may be our inferiors, but they exhibit the same qualities we possess, even if they are merely imitating us. Their management is best exemplified by an approach that treats them first and foremost as subjects of God, though blessed with lesser faculties, and therefore suited to the trade of slavery. If you cannot reconcile this approach of mine with your beliefs then I must ask you to surrender your office as my overseer. If you hold what I have crudely outlined to you to be true then you must admit that the events of last night were contrary to it and accordingly were wrong on your part. My fine is therefore fair. There is much hard repair work to be done to win the obedience of the likes of Whitechapel again. But I grant you it must be done. I remind you that your father before you did much to incur the total disobedience of Whitechapel, and you know to what specific incident I refer without me having to recollect the ghastly details. You've seen for yourself how the old man's behavior has shown over the years since your father's death, that he bears you not a shred of malice for that act perpetrated by your father against his wife. There is simply too much history between us all to justify what you did last night. Too much. What began as a single thread has, over the generations, woven itself into a prodigious carpet that cannot be unwoven. There is no good in pretending that a single thread of cause and effect exists now when in actual fact the carpet is before us with many beginnings and no end in sight. The only logical solution is to continue with this woven complexity and behave responsibly, that or we discard the entire fabric and begin again. Down that road lies chaos.

Whitechapel lost his second wife to your father. You know that. She was pure and unsullied, until he laid hands on her. Nevertheless, Whitechapel stayed with her after the birth of the boy. Sanders? Steady yourself. Your father said you knew all there was to know. He assured my father of this fact. My father took this to mean that you were fully informed. Whitechapel raised the boy as his own. In all the years he told him nothing of his forced conception. I thought you knew this. It would have been sufficient to prevent you whipping your own half-brother to death. Whitechapel should have reminded you. He must have thought you knew and did not care. All these years he kept the woman, no, more than that, loved her, put the violation behind him, made her feel she was his and not your father's chattel. She bore him no children. Not the son he coveted all his life, though blessed with a dozen daughters.

Whitechapel would not have knowingly stood back and allowed you to whip your own brother to death. He would not. You see, no one was to talk about it. And with time it sank to the bottom of everyone's minds. My father died, your father, Whitechapel's wife. It seemed all the people who were directly involved to whom it was important and painful were dead along with the shame, with the exception of Whitechapel. Whitechapel said nothing to his son. You saw the way they were together. You were supposed to know. You behaved like you knew. Deferential towards Whitechapel and tolerant of his spirited son. My orders to hold him until my return were issued in light of these exceptional circumstances.

Ordinarily, I would have let you run the plantation and hold dominion over the fate of a runaway. He was no ordinary runaway. I thought you knew. Your father was supposed to inform you and that was the end of it. No one was to raise the matter ever again. This whole mess cannot be ended any more than it can be made as simple as it may have been at its inception. Your father's action and that of countless others before him and since ensured that. Whitechapel's longevity and living memory ensures that. Our consciences, for God's sake, ensure it too. We must not allow this trade to turn us into savages. We are Christians. God should guide us in our dealings with slaves as he counsels us in everything else. Join me in a little prayer. Let us ask for advice and strength. We will pray and return to our affairs with God's grace by our side.

3

Jan 12 1796

My wife, God bless her soul, appeared in a dream and stated categorically that I had her permission to marry another. There is no other. There is no woman who walks this earth noble enough to take her place, none. I am bored with ordering disgruntled slaves around. I am bored without my wife. My son is a treasure but he is not enough.

Jan 20

My son asked how his mother died. Is it time he knew? I told him her memory was too sacred to me to discuss her death. From his contorted face he seemed more confused than anything. One day soon.

Feb 1

Who cares about my loneliness these last five years? No one. Well, God. Not enough. My son is a limited comfort. He has a way of looking up from his plate and capturing, fleetingly, his mother's look. The day was cold beyond measure and the slaves full of tricks to evade their duties. Had it not been for the cold I would have unfolded my arms more often and swung my stick on the back of their lazy legs with force. Might have warmed me up a fraction.

Feb 9

Whitechapel made a fascinating knot with a leather which when pulled untangled. He is by far the best worker, and he has the most agreeable manner. He also knows what it is to lose a wife.

Feb 16

My wife's name was on my lips. 'Caroline,' I said so loudly I woke myself.

Feb 23

Argued with Mr Whitechapel about the treatment of his slaves. He thinks I'm too severe with them. I would have kept my peace but he'd just told me that he did not want my boy running about his house because his daughter was being distracted. She is two for God's sake. They play together.

March 1

My son asked if his mother was in heaven. I answered with a resounding yes. Yes, I said, there is no other place for her if she can't be with us. He is thoughtful.

March 8
Rations of slaves to be increased along with one extra break in the afternoon following an inspection by the Master of the Whitechapel Plantation. Cock-a-doodle-doo. He said they looked thin. What good is a fat slave to anyone but himself. Mr Whitechapel you are wrong, Sir. Cattle need fattening, not slaves.

March 15
Whitechapel asked if my son was going to do my line of work. I was adamant that he was not. I think my vehemence startled him. He took a step back and showed more white in his eyes than when he smiles. Should I explain my meaning? No, not to a slave, however amiable.

March 25
Two of the older women slaves have died from fever. I am only the chief overseer here but I think it is the overfeeding that did it. They will have to be re-placed with at least one new girl. Mr Whitechapel is in complete agreement, for once. Market day next Tuesday. Will choose a girl of about 15.

March 30
I was holding Caroline in my arms. There was

nothing to distinguish waking from sleeping. This has got to stop. I feel worse in the morning than if I'd drank a barrel of beer. A barrel of beer. A barrel of beer.

April 5

I think our new girl is really a woman. I mean she must be at least twenty two. Granted, she works well. Has adjusted well to her new home. The others seem to like her. She is kind to my son. He likes her almost as much as Whitechapel does.

April 12

I told my son that we are different from slaves in intelligence and human standing before God. He asked why Whitechapel could do a knot that I couldn't do. His first joke. Not a bad one. I said doing things like that was not a proper measure of intelligence. Then he asked why they were dark and we were bright. His word 'bright.'

April 19

My old cook is ill. The new girl who insists she is 15, made a better meal than that old witch ever scrambled in a pot. Might try to trade in my old model for this new one. See what Mr Whitechapel says. It would mean buying another girl for the fields. Good cooks are hard to come by. Must be careful not to overemphasize her abilities as a cook otherwise he will want her up at his house.

May 2

My son again asked how his mother died. I said she stopped breathing because God had better work for her to do in heaven. He repeated his, 'How?'. I made him eat up. I was late for the cotton harvest.

May 9

Am I wrong to look at a slave girl and feel like a man for the first time in 5 years? I must be desperate. I need a woman.

May 26

I told the girl she was to be my cook and care for my son. She seemed pleased as any slave would be to leave the fields.

June 4

Whitechapel has struck up quite a friendship with my cook. The old dog. Twelve daughters to his name. Little wonder his poor wife died. Forgive me Caroline but it is true. The man should keep his breeches on.

July 6

The last weeks have been long days with barely time to eat, wash and sleep. My son is in good hands with this cook. Whitechapel must see her as another of his daughters, surely. He is kind, the best of the plantation stock.

July 22

I had occasion to beat a slave for indolence. Just my luck that Mr Whitechapel saw me as I booted the scoundrel. He took me aside and ordered me to exercise restraint. He said I was never to use my feet or fists on a slave again only the whip or stick. He'll be rewarding them next.

Aug 1

Today is my son's birthday. He's six. It is also the anniversary of Caroline's death. May God rest her soul. Grumpy all day. Cook baked. The house was perfumed with the smell of baking all evening. Only Caroline baked like that.

Aug 12

This cook is definitely a woman. Whitechapel does not see a daughter in her. 22 or higher.

Aug 24

Whitechapel has asked Mr Whitechapel if he can marry my cook. Damn it. Now she'll be with child for him and nursing an infant and not half as useful to my household. Petulant bastard.

Aug 30

What does Whitechapel want with a wife. Twelve daughters is enough for one man, several men. Use one of them for comfort. Not unheard of. Permission was granted by Mr Whitechapel. Their marriage ceremony is fixed for Sunday on the next convenient rest day since there is much to do. Mr Whitechapel will bless the marriage: a passage from the Bible and a smile.

Sept 5

My son said Cook made him cry when she said his mother would not come back to life. I told him that was not strictly true. He would join his mother in heaven one day. I told Cook to stick to her duties and avoid answering questions she knew nothing about.

Sept 9

Whitechapel taught my son how to jump into the air and click his heels. He was hopping between steps and doing the same thing with maddening regularity so I forbade him to do it in the house. Whitechapel, oh wise one, teach him how to stand still on one leg like a stick insect.

Sept 16

Must stop noticing the cook when she crosses a

room. She must notice me noticing her. Although I haven't noticed her noticing me noticing her.

Sept 23

Caroline was in a room with a crowd of women. I was the only man. I had my way with them all. Cook was among them. She was as sweet as the rest of them. A good night.

Oct 2

Marriage postponed again, this time until I find another cook. When I told Whitechapel his smile did not even quiver. Noble, noble.

Oct 12

Not a good stock at the market. Women who lied about their ages to pass as girls. No girls passing as women. Mr Whitechapel said something on the ride back about the clamor of the Abolitionists reaching new heights. I said on the plantation of Mr Whitechapel it was a far off din on account of his contented slaves. He liked this a lot and laughed hard and long. It was funny, but not that funny.

Oct 19

I invited Cook into my bedroom on a false pretext that there were dishes in there to be removed. She rushed in and out before I could rise from the chair. She seemed to be smiling.

Nov 2

My son again asked how his mother died. I said he would know everything when he was seven. He asked why seven. I replied he asked too many hows and whys. Evidently, this was not satisfactory, he jumped into the air and clicked his heels, twice, once for how and once for why.

Nov 10

My son said he wanted to be an overseer when he grew up because Cook said overseers were well rewarded and highly respected. I waited for him to settle in bed and summoned her before me. I reminded her about our talk concerning my son's queries. She was ready to answer. I slapped her. She sobbed like a child. I held her. Perhaps she is 15. I pushed her from me when I felt my loins swelling. Could not sleep.

Nov 17

Whitechapel asked how the search for a cook to replace his wife-to-be was progressing. I asked him if he thought he could do a better job of finding the appropriate slave to match the needs of the plantation. His smile stayed the same.

Dec 15

Christmas is around the corner. Caroline loved this time of year. I don't anymore.

Dec 24

Cook was around longer than usual. I could not concentrate on anything my eyes fell upon in *The Virginian* since I was listening to her about the house. After she put my boy to bed I waited for her to pass my door, grabbed her arm, covered her mouth and dragged her to my bed. I told her if she made a noise she would soon be dead. I was inside her and done before I'd properly begun. It has been too long. I was lying on her when her sobs brought me to my senses. I said she could have whatever she wanted from my wife's closet in return for her silence. She asked to be allowed to marry Whitechapel right away or she will tell both the master and Whitechapel, who would first kill me and then himself.

Dec 25

Cook is at her quarters. Dinner at the main house with Mr Whitechapel and his family was splendid. His wife and three children made me envious for my wife and maybe a child or two more. Should I find a wife, Mr Whitechapel wondered. We all laughed it off. Whitechapel, kill me? Sure.

Jan 1

Whitechapel married Cook today. A big affair for the slaves. He has more blood in Mr Whitechapel's stock of slaves than there are slaves unrelated to each other. What if they turned against us all?

Jan 6

Cook asked to be returned to the fields. I refused. I asked her if she has told anyone. She said no, not even her husband. I was relieved but hid that as much as I could. I reminded her that my wife's closet was at her disposal. She said she would never step into a dead woman's shoes.

Jan 9

I grabbed Cook and pulled her into my room. She fought so much that both of our clothes were torn. She bit my hand. I was an inch away from cuffing her squarely on the jaw. I resorted to choking her until she virtually went into a faint. She was a statue for the duration of what, I don't really know, since I did not enjoy myself so much as relieve myself. She cried. I promised her it would not happen again.

Jan 10

Early morning I was woken by Whitechapel, Cook and Mr Whitechapel himself. I knew their business. For a moment I considered denying everything, my word against theirs. The word of a white man is worth that of how many slaves? But Mr Whitechapel had that look I saw on his face when he came over to reprimand me for booting that lazy slave – not a look of enquiry but of resolve. I thought better of lying. Mr Whitechapel said he would fine me. He said I should spare him the sordid details and weak excuses. He said a condition of my staying on his plantation would be that I apologize right away to the afflicted parties. He said parties. The girl was one thing, but Whitechapel. Mr Whitechapel repeated his condition. I apologized to Whitechapel and Cook. Mr Whitechapel said I would have to find myself another cook, a male. They walked away and left me standing at my door. I should have cuffed her.

Jan 11

Mr Whitechapel summoned me to his house. Upon my arrival I found Whitechapel, Cook and Mr Whitechapel together. Cook revealed to them that she and I were intimate once before the last time and that the incident robbed her of her chastity. Whitechapel claims he had not touched her before their marriage. Whitechapel was not smiling.

Jan 14

More discussions with Mr Whitechapel and Whitechapel concerning Cook. Whitechapel it seems wants to give her up but was persuaded by Mr Whitechapel to wait.

Feb 10

What should happen to a woman on a monthly basis has not happened to Cook. I hope Whitechapel's fecundity prevails over mine. Mr Whitechapel said if she is with child, supposing there is a child, it is likely to be mine since the marriage was consummated between Cook's two incidents with me.

Feb 17

Another meeting with Whitechapel, Cook and Mr Whitechapel. My fine has been doubled on account of Cook's pregnancy. Whitechapel says Cook is his wife, whatever the outcome, he loves her. Everyone has been sworn to secrecy by Mr Whitechapel.

March 2

What do I say to my son? Your mother died in unusual circumstances. God blessed her with many faculties among them beauty, grace, good humor, a head for figures but not much strength. She died when . . . I can't do it.

March 10

When he is a grown man I will tell him what he needs to know.

March 17

I imagine Cook looks big bellied already. Not twins I hope. God let it be Whitechapel's, otherwise I shall have to leave this plantation, contract or no. Let the child be dark like his mother.

April 1

Caroline has risen from the dead. Cook is not pregnant just an extreme case of gas. My son wants to be a scientist or philosopher, even a poet. Ha, ha, ha.

April 20

Today Whitechapel was congratulated on the expectation of his child by a visitor to the main house who has for years been offering Mr Whitechapel gross sums of money for the slave. The man hoped Whitechapel would be blessed with a strapping son. Whitechapel's smile was broad and I think genuine.

April 29

My son recognizes some words on a page. He will read soon if he mixes a little with Mr Whitechapel's daughter who is a proper little miss. They play together at the front of the house before dusk, she has taught him counting games and rhymes which have taken the place of the usual slave songs he strains to memorize.

May 3

The slaves are never satisified. If they are not complaining about the cold in their quarters it is the wet. I had to raise my stick to several of them. They would have been better off getting my boot up their rumps instead of welts on their arms and legs.

May 12

The whole week has been taken up with the talk

about the runaway. He left before dawn three days ago. Whitechapel was interviewed on several occasions by Mr Whitechapel. All privileges have been withdrawn from the slaves and no one is allowed out of their quarters at night. The nights are long, the slaves are miserable and many of them curse the day that runaway was born. Mr Whitechapel has placed a notice in *The Virginian* with a good description and a substantial reward. I could do with that. If he comes back he will be punished. There is a lot of this mischief about.

May 27

The runaway is back. It transpires he was hiding in an abandoned cottage a few miles North of here waiting for a group of other runaways heading North, but they did not materialize. He just walked back through the main gates, looking haggard and hungry. A shame he did not allow someone to grab him a few miles out and get that reward. He got 200 lashes. I administered half, my second the rest. His back was raw. He had to be revived twice from a dead faint. All were present and seemed suitably appalled and discouraged from imitating him. Mr Whitechapel gave a rousing speech about leniency and loyalty. He got the slaves to promise an end to further attempts at escape, in return he restored their privileges right away. There was celebration well into the night. His two sons were present. One was visibly grey from the whole proceedings, the other more stalwart.

June 4

That slave who was whipped caught a fever and died. Mr Whitechapel enquired whether it was his wounds that caused his death. I said no. Apparently Whitechapel, lately changed from slave to Physician, had said, not fever, but the whip killed the runaway.

July 4

A day full of embarrassments. Cook parading with her awful big belly. Whitechapel with those know-ing looks of his and that damn smile. My son re-minding me that I would tell him about his mother on his birthday in less than a month.

July 20

Mr Whitechapel said he has found a match for me from a plantation south of here. I met the toothless, palsied hag who claims she is thirty years but must be fifty to the day.

July 26

Had a nightmare that I was betrothed to that hag from last week. Could not get back to sleep. Read from the Good Book to calm my distressed spirits.

August 1

I told my son he was big enough to learn that his mother died when he was born. He asked how old he was. I said but a few minutes. He cried all day. I should not have told him. Caroline forgive me, rest in peace.

Sept 1

Cook has given birth early to a healthy boy. White-chapel was the proud father on the plantation. He came to see me. Whitechapel showed me the boy swaddled in cloth presented to him by Mr and Mrs Whitechapel, no doubt purchased with the considerable funds held back from my pay. The child is dark and according to Whitechapel will become as dark as the lobes of his ears indicate which is much darker than the rest of his body. He resembles my son in all but colour. Maybe I imagine it. As he left I said call the boy Whitechapel, after the man he will know as his father. He bought my logic. His smile flared up again. He is so much like us.

October 5

Mr Whitechapel summoned me to his house. He asked why I had not seen the woman he went through such trouble to find for me. I said she was not blessed with many of God's attributes given to woman. He said he had a reason for his interest in this affair because it concerned the future of the plantation. He instructed me to redouble my efforts with the woman since he could not have me on the plantation a month longer if I was not betrothed. I asked him why such urgency. He replied that Whitechapel and Cook had heard rumors from a number of the slaves about the baby. Whitechapel was distracted. Cook despondent. His view was that the sooner I was married the better for all, otherwise my unmarried state would be misconstrued as a dependence on the cook for further sexual favors. He said if I left his plantation now it would be read as certain guilt and he could not allow that. He is acquainted with most plantation owners in this state and further afield and he would see to it that I never worked in this line of business again if I abandoned him.

Nov 3

I am a married man again. Whitechapel came to the house to congratulate me and wish me God's blessing of a few girl children. I practiced his smile on him but I could feel my lips trembling. Was he laughing at me?

Nov 30

My son has not taken to her. None of Caroline's clothes fit her. Thank God for small mercies. I go to bed late and in total darkness. I rise early and throw myself into my work.

4

After he laid his hands on me I wanted to die. I planned to find a way to the river whose banks were swollen and hurl myself into its strong currents. Whitechapel saved me. The second time I had to tell someone or surely die. There was no one to tell but my husband. Whitechapel saved my life. A child not his. A pure wife no longer pure. Any other man would have thrown me away. He is no ordinary man. His master respects him. I see it whenever they meet. My Whitechapel got that hound of an overseer fined. Fined. He made him apologize. And to make sure it never recurred he got him married. My Whitechapel did all that.

To think at first I shunned his attentions. What did this old man want with me but to make me a widow at twenty-five. I said no, go away, I'd introduce you to my mother if I knew where she was. Anything and everything rude I could think of. But the more insults I hurled the harder he tried. I wanted somebody young; someone who could chase my children and catch them, not this old man who would not be able to pick them up. I was wrong. He can love. He proves he loves me every day. He treats my first born as his own. We agreed never to speak again on the subject of Mr Sanders. Never. And he meant it. Not a word or jibe has slipped from him. I've seen him with that Sanders. My Whitechapel is twice the gentleman. The master is kind towards me for the simple reason that I am Whitechapel's wife and not the woman who was wronged. I know because before the marriage he did not say two words to me. Whitechapel is my life. I will bear him many sons, as many sons as he has daughters. There is no earthly way I can match his love. Every word he said to me during his visits to Mr Sanders's to see me have come true. He promised to defend my honor, to love me, to keep me by his side. Only death could divide us, he said. This I took to be idle talk; the sweetness of a man's tongue when he hungers for a woman. Not Whitechapel. How can a slave promise such things, I challenged. He said I should trust him. In another man's eyes Sanders laying his hands on me would have been a sign of my ruin. Not Whitechapel's. Another man would have seen my pregnancy with Sanders's forced seed as adequate cause to abandon me. Not Whitechapel. I will bear him many sons. He will die contented. I will grow old with my sons, alone, and happy to have met my Whitechapel.

5

CHAPEL

My father is the oldest man in the world.
I am his only son, not his thirteenth girl.

My mother is an angel without wings,
Fallen from grace, the sun has smoked her skin.

But she is lovely within; a pure light
Radiates from her; though black, her soul is white.

She is young enough to be his granddaughter
In which case I could call him Great grandfather.

He washed me with his great grandchildren,
Every day, at dusk, except on Sundays when

He supervised our wash in the morning for church.
He led us there and back with a piece of birch

Which he slapped on his left trouser leg
With each step of his left foot; us on edge

All the way there and back, afraid to laugh
Out loud and talking in whispers; I was his calf.

That birch I had to pick was never used
On me, never; it hung over me like a noose

I had no intention of putting round my neck
By behavior I knew that birch would check.

I go on about the whip because I saw
The way some children had their skin whipped raw

By parents and other adults who bore
No relation to them but saw it fit to pour

Lashes on a youthful spirit as a lesson
For later life; to teach a slave his station;

Beatings that turned children's faces from glee
To a stony obedience, all around me.

My father chose another course, that of reason.
He must have got it from seeing the master with his
    son:

How everything was either, or and maybe,
Not this is the way and this way only.

THE LONGEST MEMORY

My father said, if I could not see by
Thought how the world was and would always be,

It was a mistake for him to spare the whip,
Sweeter from him than to have my back stripped

By the loveless arm of an overseer:
Deadly, shameless, vindictive, icier.

I loved the days hanging on mother's dress.
She labored in the master's kitchen with this pest

Clinging to her hem and did nothing to shake him
    off
Or chase him from the house. She fed him sugar loaf

And watched him fatten and sang him sweet songs
And when the pest badgered her in his headstrong

Way for more, she gave more and only paused
In her song. I understood from this it was because

Of love that she did these things and I loved
Her back as much as a pest can, who strove

To emulate the kindness and love he's shown.
I learned all this in my master's big home.

My other schooling began with his youngest child.
She was three years older. She always had

In her possession soft, rectangular shapes
She peered at motionlessly for hours with no breaks.

She called them books and read aloud to me
As much as to herself, to practice and say, 'See

What I can do and you can't,' until I asked her how
For the umpteenth time and she agreed to show

Me how, if I promised not to tell a single soul.
She made me cross my heart and on a rectangle

She called The Bible, she pressed my hand,
And said swear to God. She said I had to stand

When I swore and not cross my fingers or toes
Or twitch my nose; then she opened the rose

She called a book and moved my finger over
The words as she sang them: I heard a choir.

One day she stopped me and said out of the blue,
Now you can read you must learn to write too.

My hand was a crab walking sideways
And leaving crab tracks, sideways across the page.

THE LONGEST MEMORY

Then she held my hand and the tracks straightened
As if the crab walked on two feet in one line.

I asked her to what use I could put reading and
writing.
She said I was the son of slaves and it was forbidden

For a slave to know how to write and read.
I said it was a mighty waste of a good head.

She reminded me that I took a pledge
Not to tell a soul. I watched her and felt grudge.

I bowed my head and apologized. She waved
The air to dismiss my shame. She'd saved

My place in the book; she pointed to it,
I started up loud and clear; she sat

Back in her chair and closed her eyelids;
I watched her over the top of the first words.

I must have got lost in the image of her,
Or the story of two star-crossed lovers,

Whichever, I failed to hear the footsteps
Approach and only looked round when I felt

A presence other than ours in the room.
Lydia sat up, she must have felt it too.

We gasped aloud together, the book leapt
From my lap to the floor scattering its leaves,

And we were statues with dropped jaws
Waiting for her father to release the curse

With his words. He ordered Lydia out.
He drew his belt, signalled me to bend and shout

At my peril. As he lashed, he spoke. Do not,
I repeat, do not let me ever catch you reading

Again. If you do you will be sent away,
Far away to a place where slave boys

Die of hunger, hard work and the whip.
Do you hear? For your father's and mother's sake

I hope you do. Now go to your quarters
And tell no one of this. Are you clear?

THE LONGEST MEMORY

Yes master.
I am sorry.
Thank you
For sparing me.
I promise
Never to read
And write again.
Thank you.
I am ungrateful;
A wretch,
Who deserves
To be a slave.

I promised never to open a book or pick up a pen.
I compose in my head or aloud. I write nothing
    down.

I told this to the trees, the well, the stars.
They memorized it, besides me. I told her.

He said Lydia was never to see me again.
We meet at night, back to back, without pen

Or paper. We talk. We speak from memory:
What she has remembered from books for me,

What I have composed in my head for her,
Back to back, in the darkness, at this hour.

Darkness, my father insists, anchors if
Invited into the port of an idle life.

Darkness, I counter, drops an anchor slaves
Inherit from the cradle to the grave;

It is a ship that's settled for one view;
Its anchor rusts in us; it's time it withdrew.

He said my outlook would turn my bed of straw
Into a bed of nettles with teeth of saw,

And I would nightly, still have to lie in it
With darkness as a wife, unless I quit.

He was right, I said, look where it got him.
The second the words jumped out I regretted them.

I tried to make amends but he waved me
From him and shouted at me, for the first time,

There are two types of slave, son, the first
Learns from mistakes which earn him whip and fist,

The second listens when he is told the facts,
Sees what works and what does not, then acts.

Today, I see you are the first, not second
Category of slave, and I fear for you son.

THE LONGEST MEMORY

I walked off shaking my head at the abyss
Between us; father, jailer, catalysis.

I had to leave. Mother took with fever
The weeks that kept me there, nursing her

With Father. We worked but did not talk.
I would lift, he would wash; taking turns at dark

To sit by her bed and fan and feed her drinks
And listen to her delirium; too tired to think

For myself; too mad with idle death,
Toying with the woman who gave me breath.

We were both with her when she died.
I held her head, he watched her lips. We cried

But made no sound and made no moves
Except to wipe our eyes and blow our noses.

With her gone nothing could keep me there.
Father, I am running. I feel joy; not fear.

6

PLANTATION OWNERS

I leave my plantation to face the ridicule of my peers.

You are split in two, divided down your middle by contrary reasonings. The half that argues for you to go gains the upper hand over the half that would have you collect cobwebs in the house. Before you know where you are you have donned your best livery. You insist on driving yourself in a lashing downpour to the Gentleman's Club. All the five miles you try to convince yourself you will be spared derision from men you have known all your life. The early evening air is full of whispers – rain in the trees. Sunset offers no solace.

You are heading for the club your father and his friends helped to build, to face the sons of his friends. You feel you should turn back and chain the gates of your plantation behind you, weather the shame. But you know how shame loves the retreat of shadows in order to blossom, how it cannot withstand the glare of scrutiny. The club. Your friends believe you cannot do without them and their insults because they are all you have. Of course they are wrong, you tell yourself.

My friends are my physicians, though they do not realize it. They are there to heal me.

Deeds to your plantation belong to you. There are main gates you can chain behind you. There is a threshold you need never traverse again. But you cannot live with shame.

I am a Whitechapel.

You think you do not deserve your name, yet your father's dust is between the boards of that club.

The rain has switched off. You drink laundered air. You steer the carriage over a dark blue sheet of glass spread across the road and see the sky it reflects fragment. You look up and find the sky reassembled without a seam.

Turn back, for God's sake. You don't need their mockery.

They are lions, not men, and you are driving into their den.

They see your carriage as it draws up to the club house. You climb down from the driver's seat. They wonder about the sanity of a man who owns hundreds of slaves yet chooses to drive himself in a downpour.

'Don't hound him.'

'He is a good man beneath it all.'

'We are civilized.'

They remind themselves you are one of them, however far you may have strayed.

What brings me here? My need to be ridiculed. My search for vindication. My confusion. I know the questions because I am about to ask them. The answers are mine too but I need to hear the words from a mouth I can watch.

You own the Whitechapel plantation. Your father helped to build this club. You walk through the front doors as if you are home. The floorboards under your feet welcome you with their familiar creak. Dust between those boards is yours as well as your father's. You are here because there is nowhere else. Home, the boards chatter, welcome home, as you head for the main lounge relieved of your coat, stick and hat by a slave you did not see you are so wrapped up in yourself.

You enter a smoke-filled room. Everyone is on his feet facing you. They are baring their teeth like lions.

'Here is the man with the whip in his hand. Three cheers. Hip hip!'

'Hooray!'

'Hip hip!'

'Hooray!'

'Hip hip!'

'Hooray! Well done.'

'Congratulations, Whitechapel. That was some whip.'

'Mock me all you want. It was a lesson that went wrong.'

'One long overdue on your plantation.'

The roars – louder than you anticipated – take an age to quell. There is no question of leaving, one half tells the other. A rainwater Madeira finds your hand, interrupts your search for your pipe. You try to sip it imagining it is tea that is too hot to gulp. Your throat is dry, your clothes damp. You gulp your drink.

'Slaves will see this as a warning that they can't run.'

'Or that they can run but can't hide in this region.'

'Whitechapel, you even got a mention in *The Virginian*.'

'The death of one slave does not make me one of you.'

'True, Whitechapel, true, it does not; it makes you a fool.'

'And, after all you've said, a hypocrite too. "The slaves have rights as humans; they are not just tools."'

'What about this? "Show them respect and they'll work hard."'

'"They may be inferior but they're people like us." Lost your tongue, Whitechapel?'

Roars again. Other people's smoke stings your eyes. You grip your pipe, your tobacco pouch like reins as you try to find your feet.

'I stand by every word.'

'Every last one? How do you stand by the whip's use?'

'"Slaves are humans." Whip them to death; there's proof!'

This high-ceilinged room – whose every proportion is known to you – would have you speak. You stuff tobacco into your pipe. You are offered a light by a hand you nod at in appreciation. You talk between pulling the flame into the pipe's chamber. It reddens. Smoke billows in your face. But the smoke is yours. Your eyes lose their squint.

'So none of you gentlemen has had a whipped slave die? None of you has heard of it except under my roof? And none of you has ever told a single lie?'

'I have not, Whitechapel, taken food with my slave one day and beaten him the next, or fattened him, only to have him throw it back in my face by running off no less.'

'My Christian beliefs are still absolutely true.'

'As true, my friend, as your whip on that slave boy's back that sent him to his Maker in just one stroke, no, two hundred strokes exactly.'

'I treat my slaves with humanity.'

'Give them your cruelty, perhaps then they'll survive your whip.'

'As we have tolerated your vanity.'

'And superiority.'

'Admit you felt alive for the first time in your life, Whitechapel. If not to us, then to yourself, or else you're lost.'

'Well put.'

'Thank you.'

'Well put, indeed.'

Half of you joins in the laughter. You suck hungrily on your pipe. Your glass is replenished. You are so warm your damp clothes begin to steam as if smoke issued from every pore of your body.

'Gentlemen, stupidity, it seems, comes at no cost.'

'Whitechapel is getting insulting; a sure sign of defeat. If, as you say, you can get stupidity for nothing, the capacity to insult must come really cheap.'

'What is cheaper than nothing and is still something?'

'Don't know.'

'Correct, since nothing cannot be known. One can only contemplate something if that thing already exists.'

The talk sounds familiar. You raise your glass through smoke, throw back your head, tip the last of the Madeira and glance at the ceiling made into a sphere through the clarified base of the glass.

'Whitechapel, you're an Abolitionist. We have an Abolitionist in our midst. What should we do with him, gentlemen?'

'String him up!'

You think of your dead father's warning about the subaltern nature of some of the company you keep.

'I think, gentlemen, that I am a Christian.'

'We're all of us Christians of one sort or other. But

you, Whitechapel, you promote the African at the expense of your own white Christian brother.'

'I promote the teachings of Christ and practise slavery. I do not practice slavery and hide my beliefs.'

'What you are doing will lead to our penury.'

'Or a massive slave revolt, bringing us all grief.'

'Your slaves eat well, sleep well, do wrong and get off lightly.'

'They'll start to think they're our equals and should be free. That's why your boy, dead from the whip, shines brightly.'

'We thought, at last, Whitechapel who was blind could see. But no. You persevere in your erroneous ways.'

'You actually expect us to condone your views?'

'You must be mad.'

'Dangerous.'

There is no laughter. Smoke in the air seems to warn of an imminent fire. You have been called many things.

'Gentlemen, let me tell you what it is you would have me choose.'

'Not another lesson.'

'He should be a preacher.'

'Or a politician. His constituents, slaves.'

'With a whip for a tongue; what a deadly teacher.'

Chapel. You took your belt to him as if he were your own offspring. Chapel is young, inquisitive and dead. Your policy of a judicious whip failed to save him. There is only one whip, it eats flesh.

'The corruption of the whip, gentlemen, does not save plantations; it results in brother killing brother.'

'How so?'

'What I have to say is strictly confidential.'

'Naturally.'

'We have our differences with you, Whitechapel, but honor is honor.'

'You mean it, gentlemen?'

'Whitechapel, brother, we really do.'

'Now tell us. What troubles you?'

Your head begins to swim. You see yourself wading through a sea of smoke. Smoke is above your head. Your arms tug, your legs kick but objects remain the same distance from you.

'I was absent.'

'Yes, yes. But your absence does not absolve you . . .'

'Responsibility is one thing I won't dodge. As Christians, hear me without prejudice.'

'We give you our word as gentlemen and friends.'

'We swear in the name of God.'

You chew on your pipe to steady yourself. One half tells the other there is nowhere to swim, just cloud to tread.

'The God that tells you to treat your slaves like animals?'

'Wait one minute, Whitechapel. You can't get

away with that. You are the one who whipped his slave to death.'

'Our line of work is slaves, we can't change the fact. We do it the way we think best serves our investment.'

'It's not a charity.'

'We are Christians but Christianity does not equal weakness.'

'We treat our slaves with a firm hand, we're severe in the hope that other slaves will behave well out of fear.'

'You can't mix God with the slave business. God is for us, not them.'

'You've seen their many gods. They've got one for each day of the week.'

'And every mood.'

'They can borrow our God if it will make them good. But if God doesn't work, bring back the whip and rod.'

'Whitechapel, our fathers were in this line of work. They did it well.'

'Extremely.'

'They did it for us. That's all we know. Our slave plantations put the pork on our plates.'

'And the Madeira in that glass in your hand, Whitechapel.'

'Why upset everything when it works?'

'What about goodwill to all men? And our children?'

You hear yourself and almost join in the scathing laughter that follows.

'By goodwill, Whitechapel, you mean we should free our stock. Where will that leave our offspring? It will condemn them to the white-slave auction block.'

'There has to be another way to organize the economy.'

'Other than slavery? I doubt it.'

'Slavery's fine.'

'If slaves were freed and paid they'd be friends, not enemies.'

This time you laugh at yourself. One part of you speaks, the other laughs.

'If they were free, Whitechapel, you wouldn't see them, they'd be gone.'

'Where would they go? We have money, we're here. Yet we force them to remain.'

'We're here because it suits us. They're here until we sell them. Take your man, the old slave, what's his name again?'

'The clever one his daddy named after himself.'

'The one our fathers tried to buy for twenty years. Emancipate him and you know what you promote? Demands that the plantation pay him arrears.'

'Or him in public office, giving slaves the vote.'

'Then women will want it. Then where will we be?'

'Your trouble, Whitechapel, is that you see just one part of the picture. You're so close up you can't tell the wood from the tree.'

'My slave, Whitechapel, is noble, honorable, true. He has been tested in ways that would break most men. He is living proof that slaves are our equal in every way. If you knew him better, you would know what I mean. You might change your view when you hear what I have to say.'

'Let's guess. One of your sons has copulated with a slave.'

'Or your daughter.'

'You've found a slave you actually don't like.'

'The gravity of my revelation precludes laughter.'

'We do not laugh.'

'You trust us, that's laudable.'

'Shut up then and listen. The runaway who died . . .'

'You were absent.'

'This had better be good.'

'And my overseer . . .'

'LOVERS!'

'I give up.'

You swivel on your heel. Several hands hold you, voices implore you to stay. The part of you that speaks would have you leave, the part that laughs wants to remain.

'Sorry, proceed. But, Whitechapel, you spin your tale out till the thread breaks.'

'The thread is hardly off the spool and every time . . .'

'We interrupt . . .'

'When I attempt to speak.'

'Throw us the spool, let us unravel the thread.'

'What! And get it all knotted at the outset?'

'We're educated men, not mules you have to lead.'

'Prove it and stop braying.'

'I've lost the thread.'

'That's because the end is frayed from much licking, threading and unthreading the needle. Instead of sewing the garment and finishing it.'

'All right, here's the tailored suit, fantastic or feeble. My runaway slave and overseer shared the same father.'

'You've stitched it all too fast, unpick the thread, reverse.'

'You've heard me speak of my slave Whitechapel's nobility.'

'Whitechapel! The father of your overseer!'

'There's no African in the man, he's white as a lily.'

'Is this alchemy, witchcraft, devilry or all three, Sir?'

'I show you a gentleman's suit but you see a lady's chemise.'

'Explain. We are not fools.'

'A joke's a joke. But this.'

'You knew Sanders Senior, he knew our fathers; yes?'

'Yes.'

'Well, he violated my slave's mistress. She bore the son who ran away and got the whip my overseer wielded.'

'Unbelievable.'

'Were it not from your trustworthy lips.'

'They should have known. Why were they shielded?'

'I thought Sanders knew. The whole business was shrouded in secrecy.'

'How could your Whitechapel watch and not intervene?'

'He lost a son in deference to authority.'

'Name your price. That slave of yours is a slaver's dream.'

'He's still not for sale.'

'He deserves your family name.'

'Well said indeed.'

'If he were white he'd still be rare.'

'Let's drink a toast. To Whitechapel and to his slave.'

Your glass is full, your clothes dry. The smoke you breathe is shared by everyone. The side of you that speaks is the side that laughs. You raise your glass in a sea of raised glasses.

'To Whitechapel and the old man!'

Though Chapel is gone there is still Whitechapel.

Chapel dead, the whip buried – at least on the White-chapel plantation – with him. And there is still old Whitechapel. Whitechapel, whom no grave seems able to claim, loyal beyond the requisition of duty.

At last, I am without shame. My name is restored to me.

7

LYDIA

I begin as his big sister. His hand comes up into mine and I clasp it without thinking. I lead him to a chair. This is after I watch him for days out of the corner of my eye, edging his way into the reading room. The scratching at the open door is him, half-in, half-out. I look at the words on the page and listen. What should I do? A call comes from his mother in the kitchen. He leaves this gap at the door. I listen. There is the sound of his scratching. I look around but he is gone to his mother. I must have heard the memory. The words swim on the page.

Another day he wraps his leg around the door and swings it while balancing on the other leg. The door is slightly ajar. He slips his leg around it, and begins to push and pull at it. I look at the words on the page and do all I can not to reveal my smile.

This is the day I am reading and waiting for him to appear. I half-close the door hoping he will look in the room after entering by pushing the door wide. I look at the same page and wait. Perhaps I should have left it open altogether. Maybe a smaller gap. I want him to see all he needs to see without entering the room. The thought makes me change my chair so that my body is sideways away from it instead of facing it as before. When I sit down and glance at the door I see he is there watching me. I look down at the page, breathe in deep, push myself to my feet and march over to him. He takes a step back. My smile keeps him there. I signal him to come forward but he does not move. I decide to return to my seat. In the few steps to my chair he is beside me and I feel his hand come into mine.

I sit and read aloud. He sits across from me. I look up but not much. His mother calls. He waves and scampers out of the room. I mark the page where he had to leave and close the book. I begin to read from a different book I just pulled off the shelf without reading the spine.

This is the day I decide to teach him to read, not because I want to but because he leaves his seat to stand beside me in order to look at the page as I read. I edge along to make room for him to sit. His face lights up. He perches on the corner of the chair and leaves a gap between us. I make sure he can see by leaning a little towards him. I read aloud from the usual book which I keep near to me. Next thing he is sitting properly, both legs facing the front and lean-ing over to me. His lips are moving, as mine move, without a sound or at least without a word sound since I detect the hissing noise he makes as he parts his lips and breathes through his mouth.

I take his hand, hop closer to him, so that our legs touch, and point his index finger to each word as I say it. There is more light on his face and a broad smile. His mother calls from the kitchen and he waves on his scramble out of the room. I put my finger to my lips and hiss. He nods and runs, dragging his feet on the smooth floor. I mark the page where he left off and take up another book. I read.

This is the day he says some words aloud with me when he recognizes them. The same few words. I skip them when I get to them to allow him to hear himself. He says them all with the same exhilarated voice. He is close to shouting them out. I smile and he looks away. I bury my smile for him. He is at ease again, joining in with his handful of words. His mother has to call his name twice before he hears. He runs off fast to catch up with the good boy who heard his name the first time his mother called and who is already out of the room.

This is the day he reads to me. Not a few words but page after page with occasional help from me. Now I am the one he pauses for now and again as he reads. I recline in my chair and let his voice cascade over my body. He watches me as he reads so I close my eyes to let him look without my gaze meeting his and acting as an interruption.

This is the day I open my eyes in the middle of his

reading and realize how foolish I have been. Foolish and selfish. I have taught him to read yet he cannot write his name. I open my eyes so rapidly I catch him staring at me. I sit up. He glances around thinking someone may have surprised me. Surprised us. You surprise me, I want to say, but just smile. I tell him now that he can read he must learn how to write. He nods with vigor. But before I do anything else I make him swear to keep these occasions to himself. He swears readily. He swears because he is prepared to do whatever is asked of him in order to learn. I feel awful for making him do it. There is no other way, unless we forget the whole affair, which is out of the question. I guide his hand through each letter of the alphabet and stop at W. Your name begins with this letter. Mine too. Well, my surname or last name. W for Whitechapel. His mother calls him. He frowns. 'Chapel', she says, 'Chapel', a second time, without waiting for him to answer. Then she complains loudly about always having to call his name at least twice to get a response. He does not answer until he is well clear of the reading room. By which time she calls him another couple of times. I once asked her why she abbreviated her son's name. She said because when she calls it and her husband is around both father and son answer.

8

COOK

All my life two pots are never empty. One is in the master's kitchen. The other is my own. I sometimes take from one to fill the other. Or after the sight of the first one all day, I can hardly face the second. The two pots are never empty. My master's pot is full of the best things my hands will touch but my belly won't see. Yet my pot is sweeter to me. Sweet because I take from it and fill two plates for the people I love, my husband and my son.

I am stirring my master's pot when I absently call my son. He does not hear me, though he cannot be far from the kitchen. I call him a second time. Again nothing. I turn from the pot, which can do without me standing over it for a little while, and walk from the kitchen expecting to collide with him dashing in answer to my call. Nothing.

Then I hear a voice that is my son's and not my son's. It comes from the room where the master keeps his books, a room even I have not dared to enter. The door is pushed to the point of being closed.

I put my ear to the crack and hear my son's voice speaking as I have never heard it before. He sounds as if he is standing at a pulpit or like the master sounds when he says prayers to the whole plantation at Christmas. I put my eyes to the crack and see Lydia, the darling of the house, reclined in her chair with her eyes shut. The voice of my son still sounds loud and clear. I tilt my head a fraction to the left and see that he is sitting opposite her, with a book in his hands, reading. Chapel, reading. Chapel speaking, not from memory but lifting words from a book with his eyes. My Chapel.

I have to cover my mouth to catch the scream that parts my lips. I back away from the door on my toes. My son's voice fades. Then I turn and run, still on my toes, back to my station in the kitchen. I hear nothing except my heavy breathing. A gurgling and spluttering sound drowns my breathing and I realize I am staring into the open pot of beef stew on the fire.

I steady myself before the pot where Chapel will find me when he comes bounding around the corner, then shout his name. I don't wait for his answer. I holler again. At last he answers in a voice I recognize. He runs up to me and hugs me before I can turn to face him. How quick he is on his feet these days. I ask him to fetch me some water for the pot in our cabin, the other pot that waits for me. His face is shining. His eyes are bright. 'What have you been up to?' I ask. He says, 'Day-dreaming.' 'Where?' 'Not far.' I warn him against wandering around the house and remind him that Mr Sanders's son was excluded because the master felt he was too much of a distraction for Lydia. Chapel says Mr Sanders's son only wanted to play and talk when Lydia probably wanted to study and therefore the master was right to exclude him. I remind him that his duty in this house is to assist me in the kitchen. I can't bring myself to tell him not to open a book. I can't even mention the fact that I heard him with my own ears, and saw him too, poring over a book. I want to summon some disdain before I tell him what I saw and heard but all I feel inside is pride, not fear, not yet; just pride, swelling my chest and filling my heart. My son can open a book and sound like the master. I stare at the pot and smile. He wants to know what pleases me so much and I swivel around in his embrace until I am facing him and return his big squeeze. All I say is I am happy because I have everything I could want in a husband and son.

I watch him leave. He is just out of my sight when a worry replaces him. What do I say to his father? I try to convince myself that what I saw was harmless and innocent, but I can't deny the bold, bald fact that Chapel was sitting in the master's quiet room reading to Miss Lydia. I turn my mind back to the pot and wonder what I can conjure up for the second one that waits for me to warm it, fill it, and make it sing with its sweetness. I am his mother. I can't say, 'Son, books are not for you, reading is not for you. Books will only bring you trouble. Books will only increase the number of things you have to worry about.' I will not do it, nor will I get my husband to do it. Since Chapel has kept this grand secret from me all this time in this house, he can keep it hidden a little longer. Miss Lydia. Well, well, well. Surprise knows no boundaries. I tell the pot I am sorry as if it were my husband. Husband, I love you and tell you everything, but there is one thing I cannot tell you because I know what you would do if you knew about it. You would tell my son that he cannot read – that books and slaves do not agree. You would hold up your glorious life as an example of the slave who has done all the proper things to survive and earn the respect of the master and overseer.

I can hear you, my husband. Your voice is strong and clear but without the strength and clarity of the voice of my son as he lifts word after word from the pages of a book. What I heard must not be taken from him.

The pot gurgles and splutters and goes quiet when I stir it. I think of the other pot. I plan something sweet for it. Something my husband and son will smell so far from our cabin that they will doubt such sweetness is coming from their home. But it will become stronger as they get nearer to our house and perhaps they will be forced to break into a run to see for themselves.

9

This is the day we are reading and my father enters the room and these days are brought to an abrupt end. Chapel, I call him Chapel like his mother, comes in as usual and sits. I hear the voice loud and clear without a trace of the tremor and hesitation that surrounded it when we began two years ago. At what point do I stop hearing the words and listen to the voice alone and realize I am in love with its cadence? My body is suddenly hot. The thought spins my head. It is so clear an idea that I am sure it has left my body and skips around the room in celebration. I open my eyes to see what shape my love has taken and there is my father standing with his legs apart and his hands on his hips. Chapel jumps up quicker than I. The volume of Shakespeare's plays flies across the floor and flutters several of its leaves in the air. Both Chapel and I scramble after them. Father orders me out of the room in his stern voice reserved for reprimanding slaves. I am so scared I obey. But I am more scared for Chapel. I realize I love a boy three years my junior. I realize I am in love with a slave. Chapel is in trouble because of me. Father has forbidden him to come to the house. Father tells me if I fraternize with Chapel I will surely bring calamity and shame tumbling through the roof of his house. He tells me Chapel and I must never see the light of day together, must never read together, nor write, nor sit together in the house, nor exchange written communication, nor speak of these wicked secret meetings to anyone. 'By teaching little Whitechapel to read and write when he can never use it you have done him the gravest injustice.' I want to reply that a law which says a slave should not read and write is unjust. But I look at my feet and nod when he enquires whether I have heard every word. He said it might be possible in the future. I look up at him and, as if to dash my hopes of a future when Chapel and I could sit and read together, he adds, in the next century, perhaps. I shake my head, not in disappointment but out of total despair. The next century. Chapel and I will both be with our Maker in heaven and then it will be too late. This is the world we find ourselves in. We have to learn to live with it, otherwise we will be miserable and bring trouble tumbling onto our heads. I understand, Father. I understand perfectly.

This is the day I am in the reading room dreaming, when Cook comes in. My dream is always the same. Chapel at the door scratching. Chapel with his leg curled around the door, pushing and pulling, altering the light shaped like a door on the floor and then not. Chapel in the room. Chapel sitting opposite me. Chapel on the edge of my chair. Chapel's legs touching mine. Chapel's hands in my hands. Chapel's voice washing over me. Cook said the days were getting short and short days were a blessing. I asked how so. She said they were a gift from God because of the beautiful nights when the stars shone and winked if you looked at them. She said there was a special place to sit and look at the heavens. If I go there and another person is there in that dark, she said I should not be afraid because he is there for the same specific purpose.

This is the night I go out through the back door after Mother and Father have settled in their bed. I pick my way in starlight. No shadows. The stars glow, but the shine is too weak to cast a shadow, though I imagine seeing my own, slithering beside me like a companion. I get to a place close to the house behind an old wooden shed. I think I am alone. I look up and lean on what I take to be a part of the shed. The wall is warm and gives a little before straightening again. I look up some more to allow the back of my head to find a place to rest. My head touches a shape much like its own. Do I think stars really wink, asks the voice I've missed for several weeks. The voice trembles a little but I recognize it will soon settle. Of course they wink. When a star shoots where does it land? I reply I want one to shoot now so that I can make a wish but that I cannot say if they land at all. He said the stars put out their light to avoid disturbing people when they land. He said the sound of a star landing was just like a felled tree hitting the ground. 'What would you wish, Chapel?' I can't believe I am in his company and I am saying his name. 'Chapel.' He says if he reveals his wish to me it will surely never be granted.

'How so?'

'My father told me it spoils a wish if you tell it to the person who is a part of that wish.'

'Your father is right.'

'My father is always right.'

He is more proud of his father than I am of mine. We watch the stars. My back becomes a thousand fingertips feeling his breathing. I try to match my breathing to his. We agree to meet on clear nights.

'How is the reading, Lydia?'

'Not good without you.'

'Memorize something for when we meet next time.'

'And what will you do?'

'I will compose something in my head.'

He says he cannot disobey my father. He gave him his word. He refuses my offer to bring him books and paper. He asks me to be his eyes and read for him and be his pen and write down what he says to me on clear nights. Chapel, I want to say, all my memory is yours. I ransack my head for everything I have read, but come up with fragments. He stops me and says we can start next time we meet. I will devour Father's library for you. I will leave room for your words because my head is as big as the heavens. The stars seem to get near then they join up and blur. I blink my eyes clear of the water clouding them. Chapel asks if the stars have become one and blurred.

'Yes, Chapel.'

'Don't turn around, otherwise I will have disobeyed your father. I love you, Lydia.'

'I love you, Chapel.'

We both know it cannot go on. Nevertheless we carry on with these meetings. We spend our nights apart watching the sky for the clarity we know will bring us together. On clear summer nights the cotton harvests continue until the last morsel of light is swallowed by the dark. I pray for the short winter days. Winter somehow brings more evenings than summer. At least the nights are longer. Sometimes I see stars when there are none and brave the night air. Of course he is not there, but I imagine I smell him and convince myself I just missed him.

10

I grow into a woman and know this only because others tell me repeatedly. My preoccupation with Chapel is such that I fail to see what Father truly means when he says 'young lady' instead of 'child' or 'Lydia' or 'my dear girl' and stops hugging me. Mother has started making more and more of a fuss about my etiquette, my carriage, my composure. She tells me to make smaller steps when I walk. She has me cross the room and says I stride like my father. Then she minces the ten feet marked out for this absurd exhibition and clearly her manner is false. I try to object but she insists that I actually shuffle along with my Shakespeare volume balanced on my head. My brothers and father applaud. I want to run from the room but decide to entertain them. I take a bow. I add to the Shakespeare the works of Milton and I prance the ten feet without them shifting an inch. Again there is applause but Mother shouts something about less bounce. I add Spenser to the top and try to glide across the room but only get three-quarters of the way before Spenser wobbles then slips and slides off my head followed by Milton and the Shakespeare which I manage to catch. This time there is much applause and loud laughter.

Chapel says nothing to me. Our hands explore each other's bodies in the dark. We carry on with our talk, memorizing each other's lines throughout. His hands are not so much interested in my body as curious about where the curves and downy hair end, once they begin. His mind is always set on saying the next line or getting me to repeat what he has composed and dictates to me. It may be that his hands are as busy as his tongue. The fact is, I don't recall the slightest hint of discomfort, shame or violation. The lady I have become has crept up on me.

A consequence of all this talk about my carriage as a lady is a stream of visits to the house by eminent, eligible young men. Their excuse is this or that manner of business with my father or elder brother, Thomas, but they make sure they stay for dinner or take tea when I am about to take tea and switch their talk from whatever pressing business got them to the house to me. This may sound unfair: I hold each of these men up beside Chapel to see how they compare. Not one has his wit, intelligence, charm and sensitive nature. Not one. Many of them are coarse in their humor and lewd in their suggestions which they try to dress in metaphor but only manage to drape in rags. They boast about money, acreage, slaves and their accurate pistol shot. A few mention books but only after I steer the conversation repeatedly towards the importance of libraries, literacy and numeracy. When it comes to the rights of slaves I part company with every one of them without exception. One even argued that my pretty head should not be preoccupied with the business of men and certainly not be ached with improving the lot of slaves who in their transportation from Africa are plucked from unutterable displays of savagery and barbarism.

The well which produces these streams of young men does not dry up. Eventually Father calls me into the quiet of his study and enquires after my happiness as he lights his pipe and puffs on it creating clouds of smoke that fall like a curtain between us. I say I am as happy as a daughter can be who is blessed with her health and two loving parents and brothers. He asks if my interests do not branch out further than the house. I say my limbs are still growing and I hope their reach will one day exceed the threshold of this house. Father is not satisfied. He says he is glad to hear it but wishes to see the whole enterprise accelerated. I say it is a shame to force a sapling to become a tree before it is ready to blossom. He agrees wholeheartedly but there is some irritation in his voice when he adds, between much sucking on his pipe, that there is much healthy light and food for a plant out of doors rather than in. I promise I will seek out this sustenance since it is not in the interest of a young sapling to wither and perish in the dark. I am sure I detect a frown as I excuse myself, swivel on my heels and exit in neat little strides without the trace of a bounce in any of them.

I do not feel any form of pressure until Mother starts on me. She goes through the entire list of nine young men and wants to know exactly what put me off about each one. I feign a yawn but the truth is I am seething at the imposition. She contradicts me when I say so and so was garrulous about himself without the benefit of having had a proper life to boast about, or that X's relentless treatise on money was a bore. 'Pardon me, young lady, but in my humble estimation a man who can converse is a social asset and, furthermore, money, despite all the boredom it holds for you, opens the doors to an illustrious life for a lady.'

I excuse myself from the drawing room, go straight to my room, fling myself on my bed, bury my head in my pillow and cry.

'Chapel, Chapel, I wish you could waltz into my house and hold forth in my company before my father, mother and brothers, the way you do with me. I wish you were white.' It is a miserable time to be me. I wish I could be with Chapel. I wish I were black. Am I ungrateful, God? Have I been cloistered too long in a world my two parents now wish me to flee? What can a lady of modest means do in this world without a protector, benefactor and companion? Chapel, I wish you were white or I black.

Thomas's return from the North saves me. He tells me stories of free blacks associating with white women. There is so much venom in his tone and such distaste etched on his face that I feign shock and horror but cover my mouth to disguise what might very well break out as a smile. These liaisons are open and tolerated by large sections of educated society who deplore the existence of slavery and advocate freeing slaves and paying them sums for their labor. Unworkable, impractical, idealistic. 'When they can keep their streets clean they can lecture me about slavery.'

'Yes, brother. Of course. But where precisely in the North? New York? Boston?'

I see Chapel walking arm in arm down one of these dirty streets with me. Chapel and I under the same roof. Chapel and I in the same bed.

I tell Chapel about this heaven on earth on our next meeting. He does not seem to hear. He wants something from my head I had promised to memorize but forgot to do in time for the occasion. Shakespeare's sonnet number nineteen. I tell him the previous eighteen should prove sufficient to revise in his head until we meet on another clear night. He is not satisfied. He asks me if I have been especially preoccupied by the stream of suitors at my door, too much to bother with a piffling sonnet, a mere fourteen lines, requested by one who is and remains, for all his pretensions to be otherwise, an ordinary, worthless slave. I tell him to desist in this nonsense. I remind him of the first two books of *Paradise Lost*, laboriously committed to my memory and meticulously transferred to his. I remind him of all those iambic pentameters and rhymed speeches plucked from Shakespeare's plays; of long passages from Spenser's *Faerie Queene*; of the Homer and the Virgil; of Goethe's *Faust* (Book One); need I go on? I will go on: the Donne poems; the bawdy Chaucer that made me blush and persevere for his sake; *Piers Plowman*; not to mention the hundreds of lines he composes. He puts his fingers over my lips and for the first time in our meetings he spins me around to face him, in defiance of my father's ban. He kisses me on my lips, cheeks and forehead, between telling me that he cannot live this way.

'My darling, I agree.'

I urge him to think about the North. I relate my brother's story again, this time furnishing him with every detail as it was told to me. Chapel says this journey for a lady would be hazardous, but for a slave positively calamitous and therefore unthinkable. Where would we meet if we travelled separately? How would I contrive to my parents to allow me to go North? What means would we procure for our livelihood in a place neither of us had seen before? What was the route to this place? I said I knew none of the answers to his many questions but that I could find out.

We become excited and we hug, look at each other and hug again. Then Chapel becomes despondent and lowers his chin to his chest. I take his head in my hands and lift his face to mine. I don't know how many kisses I plant on his lips but I continue until he smiles. He says he was hoping it would not come to this. That he would have to run away and disobey his father, my father and leave his adoring mother. Then he adds, without hesitation to draw a breath, that his love for me is such that no one, not his father, not my father, not the threat of the overseer's whip, nor his mother can stop him doing what is necessary for us to be together. That is it. North, here we come. Prepare to receive two new guests.

I leave Chapel and return to my room and lie awake the rest of the night thinking about how we can do this incredible thing. At each turn, I come to a wall that is too long to walk around and too high to scale. The wall says this thing cannot be done. So I take another turn and get some way along the road of my reasoning when a second wall presents itself to me and again says even this new method cannot work. I do not give up. I turn away and find a new path, one untrodden, one I work hard to clear little by little. The shutters are open. I can still see stars. They grow dim, then pale as dawn advances. Then they withdraw as the dawn unleashes the sun on a world trying to hide its many imperfections with a brilliant glow of sunlight on dew sweated overnight.

My elder brother is ready to make one of these occasional trips to the North. Thomas goes to New York and Boston to buy materials needed on the plantation and to meet with our investors and to check on our investments. I ask him if he will consider taking me. He refuses outright with that mannerism of his that betrays exactly what is on his mind in the expression on his face, in this instance, a scathing sort of dismissal in his contorted features and a general astonishment in his wide eyes that I would even dare to broach the subject with him. I swallow my rage and persevere. Can he not use me at any of his social engagements? For example, a business colleague might be with a wife, whom I could preoccupy, while he got on with business. He puts down his pen, turns bodily from his papers and, for a moment, appears to consider the originality of my suggestion, but then shakes his head negatively, saying it cannot work because it will require a lot of planning in a little time.

Next thing, Father asks me what prompts my interest in the North. I did not expect Thomas to mention our conversation to Father, thus I am taken aback by Father and have no ready answer. Nevertheless, I manage to say I have met all the men the South has to offer and, frankly, I am not impressed and think it fitting to search further afield. Father bellows at this and takes both my hands and says he is proud of my wit and intelligence and were I not his daughter and his youngest he would put me in charge of his affairs. He says if Tom agrees to it he has no objection. Then he says he can foresee no problem that cannot be surmounted, except possibly one. I ask what. He replies, my mother.

He is right. The moment Mother hears about it she says no. No, no. No daughter of hers will be sent to a strange city where the families are not known to us to risk her honor and the family name. Tom unexpectedly says on my behalf that he knows many of the best families through his business dealings with them. That will simply not do, retorts Mother. This is an affair concerning her only daughter and not some slave stock, harvest stock, trade sharehold or any such impersonal business. Then she glares at my father for some backing. Father holds his head in his arms at this point and shakes it from side to side. Mother paces up and down. Her face is vermilion. I look at Tom and William. Both cast me looks of 'Say something to calm this situation manufactured by your ambition.' I say to Mother I will do whatever she thinks fit to make this journey safe for her only daughter who is as concerned as she obviously is about her reputation and that of the family name. My brothers groan. Father shakes his head with more vigor and Mother's color deepens to crimson.

'But you interrupt me,' I blurt out. 'I mean to say, Mother should accompany me.' My brothers stare at me, Father drops his arms and looks up, and Mother stops in her tracks as if she has walked into a wall but instead of a groan she smiles. Father and Tom and Willy look at her, then they smile and then we all laugh. I do everything in my power to suppress my horror at the suggestion that has passed from my lips. I leap from my chair and hug Mother.

As far as Chapel is concerned our plan has back-fired on us. My mother will soldier me day and night until we will pray to be back on the plantation. I am annoyed at his resignation. After all I've achieved, this is the best response he can muster? I tell him he is mistaken. If he casts his mind back over the last few years, what manner of life did he see which a totally new situation cannot improve upon? He smiles, apologizes and we embrace for a long time, as if the whole plan has been laid and its exe-cution is imminent.

Tom furnishes me with as many facts as he has at hand. I am careful to enquire about accommodation in terms of my own comfort if a slave were to ac-company us. Where do slaves sleep? He said many whites travel with attendants who are accommo-dated in holdings appropriate to slaves. I ask him if it is the custom for any blacks to travel alone. He said no since they are prone to much harassment from opportunists who frequently apprehend them, rob them, beat them, and try to sell them, even if they protest they are free. I see poor Chapel in this predicament. Tom says he is puzzled by my interest in details he considers to be at the periphery of our undertaking; after all the most we will take is a woman to help Mother and me. Naturally, but my fear is that if I were to witness such a gross injustice I would be compelled to intervene on the behalf of the poor victim. He understands and hopes I would leave such acts of chivalry to him. Naturally, dear brother. So he did not need a man to help him? No, there are people at each inn who help with bags and run errands. He wants me to leave him alone. He shows this by raising both eyebrows and sighing. The expense, he adds, in this adventure of mine is considerable. Father and William will be with us as far as Fredericksburg, then we are to proceed to New York and Boston by ourselves. If I leave the planning to him and concentrate my efforts on gathering the correct clothing for the cooler climate it would be a great help. How much cooler? Poor Chapel, first highway robbers and abductors, now the weather. Considerably, is his only distracted answer as he returns to shuffling his papers.

Chapel is glad to hear about the accommodations that are available for negroes. I promise to give him money for his food. He resolves to be suitably attired. We talk about our life in the North. Childish things really. Such as at what hour we will choose to go to our bed when the necessity to meet in the dark on starlit nights is removed. We joke about associating only with other couples similarly disposed as ourselves, that is, with an equal distribution of the two races between them. Our children. We stop. The words hang in the air. Two stars that have dropped from the heavens to a point just above our heads and as bright as two suns. Our children. Yes. Our children. Several of them.

Chapel says he will write verses for a living. Verses for the birthdays of dignitaries. Verses for the death of prominent citizens. Verses to commemorate the anniversary of this or that institution or brotherhood. Verses for a gentleman to woo his lady. Verses on religion. Verses on the bounty of nature. Verses, verses, verses. And will you have the time or inclination to write a stanza or two for your dear wife? Or will you be too tired wooing the entire city of souls? There is no verse, he says, fitting to express the depth of his feeling for me. Were he to write me a verse every day for the remainder of his life, those verses would amount to one bucket from an ocean of his deep feeling for me. Chapel, you will write verses and make our lives and the lives of our children rich.

11

The Virginian

The Virginian, Editorial, December 3, 1809

It is neither extraordinary to beat a slave, nor incompatible with Christianity to wield a whip. The love I hold for God is put in abeyance during such a degrading, unavoidable act of discipline. Do not be fooled into thinking that he who holds the whip is tarnished by it. What he holds is responsibility for the destiny of several lives balanced against his need to prosper. This makes him a creature unlike any of us, simply because his responsibility is something most of us will never know. We will publicly cast aspersion at him but privately we will be glad never to have to know it. If for a day we could carry the weight of such responsibility, we would gladly be rid of it. He who wields the whip must sleep with himself. He must remember how to love. He has to lest he forget and find his hand has become indistinguishable from the whip. Then the whip cannot be put aside. Any fool can beat a foolish slave. Only a man can do it and remain dignified. Only a man.

The Virginian, Editorial, January 7, 1810

A man purchased a slave from another man who sold the said slave without realizing she was with child. Upon discovery of this fact the seller wished further compensation from the buyer for the unborn child. The buyer said he refused to pay more since the original purchase was made without prior knowledge of the fact that he was getting himself a bargain – two for the price of one.

This manner of retrospective justice cannot be argued in a court of law. Otherwise I could be charged with robbery because I ask a borrower for a certain percentage of interest on a loan which he invests unwisely and loses, when all I have done is furnish that borrower with money he would otherwise not have, at considerable inconvenience to myself. Were I to increase my interest on the loan upon discovering that the borrower has quadrupled it in a wise investment, I would be totally unjustified in doing so, since in providing the loan I had no way of knowing it would make the adventurous borrower any return. Nor would it be in my interest to care if it did or did not do so. Therefore I say to the gentleman, consider yourself fortunate if your purchased slave does not die in childbirth and the infant perish along with the mother. Ask the seller if, under these circumstances, he would be prepared to refund your money to you.

The Virginian, Editorial, February 4, 1810

If slaves are stock should we be concerned about the sale of a woman and her children that might very well result in their separation? This good question raises a philosophical enquiry into the degree of humanity we should accord slaves. Are we to attribute to slaves all the qualities we credit to ourselves as human beings? I think not.

The premise of the buying and selling of Africans is built upon precepts concerning their difference from our good selves. They are, quite literally, not like us. They do not feel what we feel. They do not value what we value. They will exhibit habits of attachment not unlike those observed among other kinds of stock on the plantation: a cow's to its newborn calf; a mare's to its foal.

It is wise not to confuse such displays of attachment and habit with love. At the auction block, get the best price for your investment even if it means breaking up the capital into smaller holdings and selling each holding separately.

The Virginian, Editorial, March 3, 1810

What is a just punishment for a slave who is a runaway? The practice has been to administer something in the region of 200 lashes with further restrictions of diet and maybe leg irons for a week or two afterwards. This seems just and fair. The assumption is twofold. One, that the runaway intended to rob the plantation of his labor for ever more. And two, that his capture should serve as an example to dissuade others from attempting such a grand theft.

If the years of service left to the plantation are calculated when that slave runs and a figure is put upon it, would it not amount to a sum of several hundreds of dollars? Even though the postulated sum is recovered upon the slave's recapture he should still be punished for the theft of his services from his master. To this end I have known overseers who had advocated dispensing of that runaway slave altogether on the grounds that he is a poison among other slaves and will himself never settle into the job again. This does not excuse the use of bloodhounds to gorge on the flesh of that slave until he perishes. Nor the use of the lash until death and then the public showing of the carcass beyond the point of decay.

It must add to the bitterness of the slaves rather than remedy any dissatisfaction in them. The key here is to punish firmly by using punishment as instruction. There is this too: the slave must be a living example of someone who has failed in his attempt at escape; he must act as a living reminder of that failure to all who might entertain such a notion. The trouble with a dead runaway, however brutal the means of death, is quite simply that the next slave soon convinces himself that he can evade the hounds and the whip and the chains.

The Virginian, Editorial, April 7, 1810

What should be done with the very old slave who has given a life of good service but who is now too old to be of much use? It seems unjust to me to simply chase him off the plantation or abandon him in some strange place as is the practice among some overseers. There must be some lighter duty around the plantation to occupy that slave.

The old slave is often a repository of wisdom to the young slave. I know of an old slave on a plantation who does nothing in the way of labor all day except shepherd the young slave children. He instructs them about the duties of obedience a slave owes to his master and in discipline and hard work. This type of old slave is an asset to the end of his days. He is a living example to the young, of the slave who can work hard and live to a ripe old age. Keep your old slaves around the plantation and see if that does not alter the general air of good cheer for the better.

The Virginian, Editorial, June 30, 1810

Young, nubile female slaves are a temptation to us all, but one that should be religiously avoided. They are blessed with youth and inspire feelings of lust in over-seers and masters alike, that are human to experience when they occur but wrong to act upon. I say this because of the offspring who have no place as slaves. And certainly they do not have a place in the house-hold of the overseer or master who has succumbed to such temptations.

If these female slaves are used in this way they en-gender bitterness in a house between the overseer and his wife or the master and his wife. The slave may even become aware of this influence and exploit it to her own advantage. I therefore argue for restraint. Couple that young female slave with a male as soon as you can to remove the sight of her and keep her busy with child-bearing. This is the sole just return of your investment in the young female slave. None other. The stories of these indiscretions always have sad if not disastrous outcomes. Two days ago, I heard of a slave who was whipped to death by an overseer, who subsequently learned the slave was his half-brother.

The Virginian, Editorial, July 14, 1810

Is Christianity incompatible with slavery? This is an old chestnut. The immediate answer is, of course, it is not, otherwise the 150-year-old practice of the latter would have driven the former from our midst. Slavery is a business. Christianity is a faith. Slavery answers to our physical and material well-being; Christianity looks after the hunger of the soul. The two are different types of sustenance for two different kinds of need. One is exterior, the other, interior. One is tangible, the other intangible.

How then are they always confused? The answer is not simple. Once we extend Christian values to include slaves we then throw into question the very basis of our forced enslavement of them. The confusion is this: the extension of Christian principles to a slave is seen as the inclusion of that slave in all aspects of our Christian life. This view is wrong. It should be possible to *treat* a slave with Christian fairness and *instruct* him in the Christian faith as a just substitute for his pagan practices, without nullifying the relationship of master and slave. It has to be. Otherwise Christianity could not be spread. Otherwise the African would be deemed our equal simply because he shared our faith in one God and the Afterlife. We know both of the above to be false because of the evidence of how Africans live in their primitive land. For God's sake remember where they came from before you thrust them upon an equal platform with ourselves.

The Virginian, Editorial, August 4, 1810

How should the plantation be run, firm or kind? Those on the side of the firm argue that it keeps slaves in their place and at a suitable distance from the Master and Overseer. This distance they argue facilitates the smooth running of the plantation.

Those on the side of the kind approach point to the number of runaways on the firm policy plantations as evidence of the failure of the whip and stick, stock and chains, bloodhounds and general abuse. They argue for a good diet for slaves instead of keeping them hungry; good dry shelters instead of hovels even the bloodhounds would not be housed in; fair amounts of rest from work to facilitate an air of hard work equals good treatment.

The kind approach says what is called firmness is often inhumane and unnecessary practice against slaves. They say profit is not increased by it. Let me declare I am somewhere in the middle of these two extremes. As a businessman I can understand that some aspects of the firm approach, such as, harsh punishments for runaways and indolence, are essential. As a Christian it seems only right to reward hard work and provide a minimum standard of comfort. If that comfort can be assigned to bloodhounds then why not slaves?

The word is neither firm nor kind in my view. The proper word is *fair*. A fair approach to the resolution of all problems on the plantation on the basis that the interest of the plantation is uppermost on the list of priorities. The lot of the slave need not be miserable.

The Virginian, Editorial, September 1, 1810

I was asked if slavery will ever come to an end. Clearly my answer was going to be of critical importance to the questioner who wanted me to answer in the negative unhesitatingly. Much to his consternation, I took my time. I said to him, after a long pause when I stared at the heavens, that his question had a yes answer (at which his face fell) and a no answer (at which his expression became gleeful) and asked him which did he care to hear first.

He said the negative. I said that in so far as man's labor will always be required in the cotton, corn and tobacco fields, to name some, I could see no end to slavery.

In reply to the affirmative, I said the world was changing rapidly. 150 years of slavery was a long time. Advances in techniques for manufacturing goods must at some stage influence the work of slaves and result in much cheaper ways of doing things.

How soon, he wondered. I said, not in our lifetime nor that of our children. This cheered him up mightily. He shook my hand and strode off as if I'd written a decree outlawing any interference with the institution of slavery. The long stretch of time I quoted for its demise was reason for his jubilation. It is not. The growing numbers of freed blacks in our midst is one indication of this.

The Virginian, Editorial, May 5, 1810

An intriguing question was put to me by a reader who requested that her identity be kept a secret. So I shall use the initial of her first name, L. Miss L. wondered if it would not be more profitable to *pay* blacks for their work instead of keeping them as slaves and having to provide for *all* their needs in exchange for their labor. This seems laughable to many upon first hearing of it but it does merit further consideration. I did some calculations and came up with the following. If I understand Miss L. correctly she means by 'hire', a sum paid to the black just for his work in a market where the price would be set according to how much *need* was placed on that labor. This is not a fixed cost. If say there are 500 free blacks and five plantations need 100 each then the owners of those five plantations could conceivably decide between themselves *before* hiring, what they are prepared to pay each hired black.

But if the same five plantations wanted 150 slaves each they would have to compete among themselves to attract that labor. The inverse is true if only 50 slaves were needed for each plantation out of a quantity of 500 slaves. On some occasions it would work for the blacks, on others for the plantation owners. It all sounds too rife with variables to be practical though I grant you it is an intelligent question from a lady. Thank you Miss L.

The Virginian, Editorial, May 12, 1810

Miss L. has properly pointed out to me that my editorial in last week's edition wrongly gave the impression that slavery was a static and stable institution, whereas her proposal was wild with fluctuations. She argued that she has witnessed an escalation in costs at her father's plantation without a corresponding increase in profits, both of which indicate to her delicate mind that slavery is a growing expense and the returns from it a diminishing one.

Miss L., your father's plantation is only one example, though I am sure an excellent one. The rising costs may have more to do with inefficiency than some natural, inevitable escalation. As for your point about diminishing profits, you will find that the pattern is true for most plantations in the present depressed climate. We can only hope for an upturn at a date not far from now. I must say Miss L. this does not place slavery on the same slippery foundation as your open market system; nor does it indicate as you seem to believe that slavery is dying as an institution.

Thank you for your correspondence.

THE LONGEST MEMORY

The Virginian, Editorial, May 19, 1810

An astonishing thing has happened that forces me to think of changing the policy of this paper. I'd assumed that these humble pages were read by educated white Virginians alone. It transpires that there are literate slaves in our midst who read this paper to themselves and aloud to slaves who cannot read. One such slave has written to me in the most articulate letter I have received in a long time. In it he argues that these pages should carry stories about slaves told by the slaves themselves. It is a point worth entertaining. In past debates in these pages it might have benefited some of the arguments if the point of view of the black were heard as well. I would have printed the letter but it is dictated to some undisclosed person who has written it on behalf of the slave. In addition, the policy of this paper is not to include correspondence from slaves.

It occurs to me that not using his own hand to write the letter may have been an attempt by the slave to get around this policy. Perhaps not. The literacy of slaves is generally frowned upon, nay positively discouraged in most quarters. I am of the opinion that if it benefits the plantation to have literate slaves then so be it. By the same token if it benefits our readers to hear the viewpoint of slaves and free blacks alongside their own then so be it. Write in with your opinion on this matter.

The Virginian, Editorial, May 26, 1810

The overwhelming response to last week's question concerning the literacy of slaves and the inclusion of their thoughts in these pages was a resounding, 'No'. As an indication of how this matter can divide families two responses came from a father and his daughter who wrote in separately. The father said no, definitely not. The daughter said, yes and about time. The father said it filled a slave with discontent when he can read about the world but must live on a plantation as a slave and see nothing of that world. He added it was unethical to instil in a slave such an outlook and he went so far as to claim it was detrimental to the workings of a plantation. His view was upheld by the vast majority of readers.

The minority view is nevertheless deserving of some discussion. As outlined by the daughter, it argues that it is wrong to decide what a slave should and should not know and doubly wrong to rob that slave of the joys of literacy. She said it made slaves better people. In fact, she advocates literacy for all, since, in her view, it would improve mankind.

Whatever we may think of this young lady's opinions we must grant that she demonstrates intelligence and certain advantages that go with being young, namely an unmitigated idealism. This is as it should be. It is the young, after all, who hold dominion over the future.

The Virginian, Editorial, June 2, 1810

A deputy to an overseer has written to me saying too much attention is paid to the plantation owners and to the slaves at the expense of that level of poor whites who have to work for the former in close proximity to the latter. He argues that the lives of some of these whites are barely one rung above that of sharing the condition of the slave. Furthermore, many free blacks with a trade live and eat better than these whites. That cannot be right he laments. Moves to emancipate growing numbers of slaves exacerbate the already awful situation of these impoverished whites.

He issued a threat which it is not in my normal practice to heed or publicize but which had a particular vision of the future that made me think I should make an exception on this occasion. In his view these whites will rise up and exact such a revenge on the blacks that none will be left to see. He does not stop there. They could very well turn upon those rich whites who have ignored the plight of their poor brothers and treated them as if they were merely blacks who were free.

The Virginian, Editorial, June 9, 1810

Many readers agreed with the outlook of last week's featured letter. Many felt these whites were the forgotten *stratum* of society. Some confessed that they had had first-hand experience of the treatment of the free black when they tried to get work at a plantation. They were either sent off with a rude word or dismissed out of hand when their services were no longer required. There is no excuse for employers to treat the labor they need to hire as if it were slave labor. It is not. The differences are many and important. Though obvious, they are in clear need of reiteration.

One is free, the other is not. One is white, the other black. One comes from the less fortunate portions of our ancestry, the other is not our equal nor derived from our race. The interests of these whites should therefore supersede those of the slaves and free blacks whenever the two come into conflict.

I do not subscribe to the vision of a violent future if the interests of these whites continue to be ignored. I do not for the simple reason that their Christian faith will act as a restraint. I certainly do not see them attacking their own kind however wide the gap between their need and the other's privilege becomes.

The Virginian, Editorial, June 16, 1810

There is no sight more perfidious than that of a white woman with a black man. I was in New York and witnessed examples of this and left appalled and enthralled that my home was made here in the verdant hills of this blessed State where no such displays are ever likely to occur.

There is so much wrong with it and it is so far from us here that I should not grace the idea with any further discussion. But there is something in it that did not augur well for the future in these bounteous United States. Namely, what will become of the offspring from these heinous alliances? Where is their place in these States when they see themselves as our equal and *feel* it too because the blood courses through their veins?

The same argument applies to masters and overseers who satisfy their concupiscence on slaves without due consideration of the consequences. I grant that the latter are born as slaves and therefore come to know their station and are less of a problem than those who are born free and then have to learn that they are not and live with that.

The Virginian, Editorial, June 23, 1810

Miss L. wrote in and called my thinking on last week's issue concerning the perfidy of liaisons between white women (they are not ladies) and black men unconstitutional. The writer did not say whether my condemnation of the same behavior in whites, namely, masters and overseers, towards black women was also unconstitutional. Nor did the writer comment on whether my vision of their offspring as posing a problem for society was similarly unconstitutional. I suppose it is unconstitutional to warn against practices that harm the smooth working of a country. Perhaps it is equally unconstitutional to wonder where it will all end.

Miss L. is a previous correspondent who has brought reason to this column in the past. I credited her at the time with intelligence. I see now I was grossly mistaken. She exhibits a love for blacks that clouds her ability to reason about any subject involving them. Her thinking puts her in that bracket of females who end up in the North walking arm in arm down a dingy street with a black man. Should this occur, at least she will have been the mistress of her own fate, which is, I will allow, as constitutional as a person can get.

12

GREAT GRANDDAUGHTER

'New England lice bite harder than African lice.' He dropped this in his little talks with me as he supervised my wash. 'Do behind your ears,' I hear him say. 'Now under your arms. Use plenty of water. Good girl. You will grow up to be beautiful and strong. Now between your legs. More water. There's more where that came from.' He made me fetch the water for my wash with a bucket in each arm. 'A clean child is closer to God than a dirty one,' another one of his sayings. I asked him what African lice looked like and how New England lice managed to get all the way to Virginia. He said he left Africa when he was a boy. One day he was playing in a field of tall grass. The smell comes back to him all these years later unannounced. The next he was marching. Several days after that he was facing the sea for a journey he thought would never end and one that claimed many lives, young and adult. No one lifted a finger to help a ten-year-old boy. Women and men were like children in the hands of those who held them captive.

And the lice? The lice in Africa do not bite, they tickle. Children like being tickled so they carry lice on them. If they do not have any they hunt for some. Without African lice on their bodies they are sad. New England lice by contrast have teeth. They bite pieces out of you and drain your blood for sustenance! If I washed with plenty of water I'd keep them away. He stopped supervising my washes when he asked me to scrub my chest and I told him my nipples hurt. 'Go wash with the women.' But I wanted him to be there. He was African Great Grandfather to me.

I told him I had a dream about Africa. He said, between supervising which part of my body I should wash next, what did I want to go and do something silly like dreaming about Africa for. I had plenty of water left and my knees, elbows and feet still to scrub so I told him my dream anyway. I fly through the air and land in a place I know is Africa. The first thing I do is kiss the ground. I get down on all fours and kiss the soil or sand which feels like something I could eat and not get a belly ache. My kiss is not a peck or a brush of the lips but a full-mouthed kiss so that when I rise there is a ring of soil applied to my lips and I don't care about it. That's how I know I'm back where I belong. I shade my eyes from moonlight turned sunlight without warning and duck into a hut just as bright with firelight. I stay inside in that glare even though it forces me to hold a salute over my eyes, first with my left then with my right hand. I soon grow accustomed to the brightness and make out the figures of family and friends slapping me on the back, squeezing my hands as if to wring water from them and kissing me, kissing me on the mouth in such quick succession I pant for air which the repeated slaps on the back and bear hugs squash out of me.

A pot on the fire in the center of the hut gives off a smell of pepper and spices that turn my mouth into a spring. Where people once stood, they sit, ready to eat. I have to swallow every few seconds to stop myself from dribbling over the contents of this pot. A steaming, heaped clay plate is thrust into my grip and I am pushed from my feet to the ground. Everyone motions for me to eat. They don't take from this glorious pot but stop to watch me. I think it may be some potion that will turn my head and leave me helpless and in their clutches but I don't worry about that thought. I scoop up a handful of something that resembles rice and a meat I don't recognize. I taste sweet, sour, salt, rolled into one. A big cheer from everyone threatens to lift the roof off the hut. Someone next to me holds up my left hand, the hand I do everything with and says, 'This is indeed the great grandchild of our son.' I realize they mean you Grandfather: your left-handedness that nearly all of us have inherited. The room begins to spin. Flames under the pot lose their shape. Heat all over me makes me feel as if I'd taken the place of that sweet and sour pot above those flames. My grip loosens on the plate, spilling the meat and rice into my lap. I jump up and I'm awake shouting, 'I am the third grandchild of his twelfth daughter: his youngest great grandchild.'

'Africa is not for you,' was all he said in response. I asked why. He poured the last of the water over me. His signal for me to leave. I did not do my usual dance of rubbing all over my body in a hurry. I stood there shivering in the dusk. He looked at me with his raised eyebrows as if to say, 'Are you challenging me girl?' I looked at my toes burrowing into the ground that I wanted to open and close over me, yet I stayed rooted there waiting for him to say something. At last he impatiently replied, 'Because you don't recognize the food.' He flicked me that look of 'get out of my sight girl', but I returned him knitted brows. He read my puzzlement.

'You dream about something you don't know. Make your dreams here.' He was annoyed with me for dreaming. Well, I didn't like what he had to say. He never talked about Africa. It was his view, I found out later, that such talk promoted day dreams and insolence on the plantation. He said Africa was his past and not ours. If anyone had the right to dream about it, he did and he chose not to, so why should anyone else.

He always said 'great' when I called him Granddad, but so quiet I would just catch it. I stopped calling him Granddad to stop him saying 'great' every time.

The few occasions I forgot and called his name he had his 'great' ready for me. He had married again after years on his own. His son was younger than I. As a matter of fact his wife was younger than my oldest sister. But she acted older, and, for a while, made Granddad sprightly again and brought back his smile. Her death took away his smile, turned down his mouth. His son's death deadened his eyes, and because he caused that death we all run from him, except my brother who ran into him and has a permanent swelling on his forehead as a result of the collision. No one speaks to him or smiles at him, except me, sometimes. When I walk past him in a wide arc he sits down. It makes me laugh. I fight back the laugh but it shakes my body. He is a ghost we all see and ignore because he killed his only son.

When his son was missing, a great conference began about what would happen and what could be done. Grandfather announced his intention to tell the master where his son had gone. He said it would bring him back in one piece. I and everyone else failed to see how betraying his son's whereabouts to the master he'd escaped could be construed as a protective act. Everyone, without exception thought the old man had finally taken leave of his senses. He held up his hand and said each of our names. He said there were things he knew which he could not impart to anyone. There were calls of, 'what things, what things?' His final plea was for us to trust him in this decision concerning his son whose well-being was uppermost in his mind. With that he turned from us and we parted like the sea for him. There was some talk of restraining him as he strode towards the big house as if he owned the key to the front door, but no one moved.

Everyone was ordered to the yard. We were all eager to go, not to watch a beating that should not be happening in the first place, but to see the face of the old man who made it possible. He behaved as if the whole incident were a surprise. I saw how the whip exacted as much of a toll on his aged body as his son's. From that day I could do nothing for him. I smiled. I called him names but I could do nothing for him. I had seen and felt the result of his actions. One of us was absent because of him. He shrank in stature before my eyes. From his habit of sitting down un-accountably it was clear any manner of attention had become better than none at all. I wanted to fetch his water for him and help him bathe.

My dream about Africa? Gone. Banished to the place where dreams retreat when they are ridiculed. In its place are nightmares.. Of a beating that never ends. It wakes me. The whip keeps a slow time beaten out on a man's back. This man is quiet, so quiet I peer to see if he is living through what is hap-pening to him as much as me. His mouth hardly grimaces. His eyes are like his father's would become from that day: still, dark and detached from his body.

His mouth responds to the whip as does his body, contracting with each lash then relaxing from exhaustion. I see from his eyes that he is absent from himself long before the end. This is good.

What form of reasoning could have convinced Grandfather that his son would be safe? I have wanted to ask him every day since, imagining I could defy the ban to speak to him, and be damned myself because what Grandfather would tell me would be infallible. But all I did was call him Sit-down Grandfather, see him mouth the 'great' I always leave out, and dream about helping him with his bucket in the walk up the hill from the well and pouring the last of the water on him so that he could use both hands to rub himself all over.

His body is stiff. He lies half-curled. His skin is already cold. I start at his head, his face, neck and behind his ears; wiping the slack skin in his neck to catch a streak of water, wiping the set creases at the corners of his mouth. Then his hands. I uncurl the fingers which have the resistance of the dead in them and wipe the palms with their pathways of an ant's nest. His knuckles are round as stones. His nails are as dark brown as his skin. I cannot carry on. I am led from the room and the ablutions are continued by another of his great grandchildren. It would have been easier to fetch his water and pour it on him, leaning forward on the balls of my feet to avoid the windmills of his arms and the spray.

13

SANDERS JUNIOR

Uncover him. So you are really dead, old man. You look like you could be taking a nap. Not dead. I really thought you would outlive us all. Not curled up like this, tight as a nut in a shell. Peaceable. Like you've sneaked off into a quiet corner for one of your catnaps in the middle of the day. That's what kept you living so long, I bet. While the rest of us were busy sweating in the sun you were nowhere to be found because you were curled up like a cat in a woman's lap. Except the lap is the hard ground. We'll bury you here, old man. I like you, though I struck you with these very hands. I'll dig your grave. I hit you because you didn't know when to hold your peace. I shouldn't have hit you, but you contradicted me in front of everyone. My status as overseer was undermined before the slaves who needed to see it reasserted right away. So I hit you. You will recall it wasn't hard. There no blood. You hardly swayed. If you rocked back on your heels it was to avoid the impact of what you wrongly guessed would be a fist.

I couldn't strike you. You showed me how to run things. My father spoke highly of you. You were a better overseer than I. There I was, thinking I was the first one to rise in the morning, setting an example for everyone, and you were out here even before me. Always first and last in everything. I am sorry about your son. Not my brother. I knew him only as the son of a slave. He was trouble from the day he talked. He not only asked questions but when you gave him an answer he was never satisfied. He always asked why: Why this? Why that? That's the way things are, that's why, and neither you nor anyone else is going to change them. No matter what you say or do. So do your job and I'll do mine and things will be fine. But no. Not your headstrong son. He couldn't have been yours. I know that now. He did not demonstrate an ounce of your common sense. His spirit was wild, yours tame. His manners uncouth, yours impeccable. I see nothing of my father in him. Nor of myself.

What did you do wrong, old man? To raise a son whose nature was so contrary to your own! All those years taught you nothing. Only you could have stopped him from running. Only you could have saved him. You knew he might run. We all did, but chose not to believe he would actually do it. Not after all the threats from me, my deputy, even Mr

Whitechapel. 'Too many instances of runaways not being found', were Mr Whitechapel's words. Too expensive. Too much of this planted seeds of discontent on the plantation which sprouted anarchy. The next man to leave the plantation without due authority to do so would be made an example of by a public whipping. Mr Whitechapel even specified the number of lashes – two hundred. Said he'd read it in *The Virginian* in reply to a query from one of the readers about a just punishment for a crime that was becoming a plague on the plantations and would certainly kill them off in their entirety unless the plague were treated in a swift, decisive manner. Two hundred lashes it had to be. He was warned. Even if you had shouted to me that I was killing my half-brother I would have had no choice but to carry out the punishment. Of all the young slaves he was the one deemed most likely to run away. You remember we even confined him to duties closer to the house where an eye could be kept on him? You were assigned to watch him. The man who never shut his eyes. How did he slip out of your sight? What could I do? Mr Whitechapel did issue orders for me to wait, do nothing until his return, but what do you think he would have said? 'Release the dear boy'? We were right all along. We said he'd run and he did run. Should I have rewarded him for it with three square meals a day and the lightest duties on the plantation, just like his father? Mr Whitechapel may have reduced the number of lashes. He may even have said, 'Go light on the whip.' But the punishment would have happened. Of that I am certain. This is a business, not a charity. You don't work for your own living. You work to make Mr Whitechapel richer. Your lives aren't yours, but his. My father's son, the son you reared, forgot that. Granted, you never did. You knew your place, old man. I like you for that.

What a child's way of sleeping you have, curled up, neat as a nut. I tried to catch you sleeping during the day. The one time I crept up on you and I was certain you were asleep you opened your eyes and winked at me. My stick was raised to deliver a stinging surprise to you, but that wink of yours froze the stick over my head until you straightened up on your feet and wobbled away without a word. You vagabond! Full of tricks paraded as innocence. Death got you though. You had nothing up your sleeves when it came to death, so you just lay down and curled up and died. Now I'll bury you. You'll get a grave with a stone. You were a slave until death, an example to your race. Centenarian, you look like a child now. Cover him and move him into the barn. It's cool in there and quiet. Wake everyone. Tell them the old man is to be buried this morning before their duties. I'll tell Mr Whitechapel. He'll take it badly. He liked Whitechapel; thought as long as he was around the plantation would profit. What's supposed to happen now? Superstitious nonsense. Whitechapel lived long, that's all. There's no mystery. Some men are born strong, others weak. Whitechapel was strong. What did he do with his life? Slave. A good slave, but a slave however one chooses to look at it. I wouldn't want to live so long as a slave. I don't want to die alone, in the open, with nothing to my name.

Don't move him without covering him first. He was a good man. Cover him with my jacket. I offer it to you, old man, in death. I could never offer it to you while you lived. No law said I couldn't, it just isn't done. I am sorry, I did not knowingly kill my half-brother. He was weaker, more tired than I thought. I did not want him dead, just a lesson taught to him for all to see. That's all.

You are curled like a nut in a shell but you must have been cold before you couldn't feel the cold anymore. My jacket is too late to warm you. It covers your whole body, old man. I want him buried in that jacket unless his people object. Keep it on him, you hear. It's as old as him. It belonged to my father. Whitechapel was the only man besides me who worked alongside him, and remembers him. What would my father have done? He would not have countenanced any of this, I'm sure. What I did to your son was an emulation of my father's likeliest action had he been in the same situation. He advocated a firm hand, always. He said ambiguity towards a slave was taken as a sign of weakness.

Privately he disagreed with Mr Whitechapel but carried out orders. I am his son. I think like him. You yourself said I resembled him, that I was my father's young self. But my memory of him is sullied. He lacked your courage, Whitechapel. If you were white I would have wanted you as my father. The jacket is rightly yours. Damn it! Keep him covered!

FORGETTING

This is what I imagine saying to him. My son, you have to answer the call of your blood. You were born half a slave, half the master of your own destiny. You shake your head at me because you can see only part of my argument. The rest of it takes you from me. I know that you belong to another way of life. Yet I tell you everything I know, everything I see and hear and work out for myself, as a slave. I tell you because I must. It should suit a son of mine, born a total slave. But not you with your blood. What I say can never be enough for you. I want to keep you alive, that is all. I do not care about your happiness; your life is everything to me. I fail you as a father. I am insufficient. All my years are insufficient.

What you shout in your sleep is a young man dreaming. I hear but pretend I am deaf. Her name is a young man dreaming. Lydia. A dream of love, desire, but a dream all the same. Something that cannot be possessed; that will remain confined to the realm of sleep, fantasy. I think it is healthy that you express signs of desire, manhood blossoming in sleep. Once awake it will take a different form I tell myself, one suited to your life, your circumstances. I see now that the name Lydia is a part of the dream you tried to make a part of your life. To choose. To have. To keep. Lydia is a part of it. Which part I do not know. I am wrong in many things. Shall I tell you about your blood? That two races are distributed evenly in it? Shall I help you prepare for a life elsewhere? Where? This is the only place I know. Maybe I am wrong, I wonder to myself, as I see myself doing it, wrong to tell the master that my son is gone and say I want him back under my guidance and protection. Then I ask myself, after I see the entire scene, what guidance? What protection?

All the time you are listening to your blood and following the dictates of your dreams. 'Twelve daughters,' I hear myself say to someone who is impressed to hear it, then I tell myself, as if I must counter this good thought with a bad one, yet I cannot rear a son, one son.

I have been wrong all my days. I am an old man. My skin is tight over my joints, so tight it shines, even at night. Elsewhere on this body, skin hangs as if about to drop off, or gathers, creases and cracks, and looks more like the muddy bottom of a dried-up river than skin.

Too much has happened to put right. I would

need another life. No, several lives. Another hundred years. No, more, to unravel this knotted mess. Too tired even to begin. Wouldn't know where or how. Maybe what's done is done. It cannot now be undone, only understood. Others might understand. They will look and see a man who has too many days and nights. They will see a time when a short life was the best life to live under such conditions. The master is daylight, the slave is night. A complete day needs both light and dark. The day cannot be broken in two to leave each half to itself. Nor can the master hope to rule the day and the night along with it forever. Slavery is a long day of the master over the slave and of nights turned to days. But how long can the master's daylight continue to rule our nights?

My head is too heavy for these shoulders. Eyes that have seen too much for one body, rest. Mouth that has kept too much to itself, utter. Night and day these eyes are open. Night and day this mouth refuses to speak; cannot begin to speak; has too much to say. The mouth turns down. All the things it has never managed to say have soured there. The lines deepen in time. The eyes deaden. Gradually losing light to darkness. Looking without bothering to see; staring but reacting to nothing, however dramatic, personal, grand, final. The eyes see their own death and do not flicker. The mouth tastes death and does not move. Death has always been there. Death brings more sourness. Mouth is almost pleased to recognize death as a lifelong companion; something always present in those sour corners. Eyes feel the same. The light going out is death's shadow; death sitting up suddenly behind the plate-glass of the eyes.

I must sit down. No, lie down. Rest these eyes, tired of trying not to see. Rest this mouth. Stop tasting the sourness there. Forget. Memory is pain trying to resurrect itself.